Leather Family Dynamics

"'Aunt' Grace" -- Jen needed a place to stay in Portland and turned to her father's stepsister. But, she found so much more than she ever dreamed possible with her "Aunt" Grace. Second Place, National Leather Association: International John Preston Short Story Award.

"Leather Family" -- Kyle needs his own boy. Jacques would do almost anything to find a place in a Leather Family. But, Kyle serves a female Master.

"Searching"-- Two dominants love each other, but need someone who submits to them both. Just how far will young Jesse go to serve the lovely Lady Theresa?

"Taking Control" -- To free the woman she loves from a horrid sadist's perverted games, Melanie must set aside her own aversion to men.

"Family Ties" -- When her slave's ex faces eviction, Katherine offers refuge. But can Naomi pay the price?

"Said the Unicorn" -- Tessa dedicates herself to her Master's service, so his determination to add another woman to their family devastates her.

I.G. Frederick trades words for cash, specializing in erotic fiction and poetry since 2001. Her erotic short stories appear in Hustler Fantasies, Forum, Foreplay, and Desire Presents, as well as electronic, audio, and print anthologies. Her novels receive high praise from readers, critics, and other authors.

A FemDom, Ms. Frederick, owns the man she adores. Although dominant in the rest of his life, he demonstrates his love by serving as her submissive. Ms. Frederick often writes about finding love in BDSM relationships from the authority of one enjoying that for almost a decade.

http://eroticawriter.net/

Leather
Family
Dynamics

Includes
NLA-I
award
winner
"Aunt" Grace

Six Sultry Stories Explore
Sexuality in D/s Liaisons

I.G. Frederick

Author of Dommemoir and Lessons Learned

Family Dynamics
© **2014 by I.G. Frederick**

ISBN: 978-1937471-15-6

Pussy Cat Press
http://pussycatpress.com/publisher.html/
P.O. Box 19764
Portland OR 97280

First published electronically as *Family Dynamics* in 2013
Name changed because of Amazon's arbitrary and capricious "content guidelines."

"Leather Family," first published as "Family," in Xcite Books
Her First Submission and other stories, September, 2011

Slightly different version of "Taking Control" first published
as "Three Way," in Xcite Books *Lesbian Love 3,* May, 2010

Table of Contents

"Aunt" Grace

By I.G. Frederick
and Patrick

Weeks had passed without a response from Aunt Grace. As fall term drew closer, panic chased away Jen's excitement about her acceptance to the Art Institute's game design program. If she couldn't find someplace in Portland she could afford, she'd have wasted the last two years of her life.

Her cell played the *Silent Hill* theme and Aunt Grace's photo flashed on the screen. Jen swallowed hard and prepared to beg.

"Jen, hi. Sorry I haven't gotten back to you sooner. I had to give some thought to what you're asking." Leave it to her father's stepsister to get straight to the point. "When'll you be in town? Can we meet somewhere and talk about this?"

Jen tried to keep trepidation out of her voice. "Fall term doesn't start until next month, but I was thinking about taking the train up this weekend."

"Great. I'll take you out to lunch. How about one thirty on Saturday. Meet me at Hamburger Mary's, on Fifth just south of Couch, it's only half a mile from the station."

Jen stepped off the bus and heard the conductor hollering, "Board." She dashed for the train and climbed into the car as the whistle blew and the locomotive lurched to a start. Finding an empty row, she set her backpack on the aisle seat, pulled out *Game Over*, and tried to read. But Grace's reticence about Jen's request to live in her spare room for the next couple of years made it impossible for Jen to focus on the words.

"Whatcha reading?" a male voice asked.

Jen didn't bother to look up. "A book."

"I suppose you're too high and mighty to carry on a conversation with a fellow passenger?" The stench of beer breath invaded her space.

Jen turned another page.

"Did you buy a second ticket for this seat? One to a customer, ya know."

Out of the corner of her eye, she saw the man's hand on her backpack. In one practiced move, she grabbed it and used it to push him out of the way so she could flee up the aisle. "You want the seat, you can have it," she shouted without looking back.

She could hear footsteps behind her, so she slung one strap over her shoulder and picked up her speed, grabbing seat backs to keep her balance against the train's swaying. She found the Bistro two cars back and spotted conductors seated at the far end.

"Can I sit at this table?"

A stout grey-haired man with his hat on the table next to him shook his head without looking up from a pile of forms.

"Please, another passenger is harassing me."

A short, slender woman in her early forties, also wearing a conductor's white shirt, dark tie and slacks, stood up. "Here, hun. Sit inside. No one'll bother you if you're not on the aisle."

The older man glared at her, then returned to his paper-work.

Jen spotted Aunt Grace at a small, square, wooden table near the brass rail separating the bar area from the restaurant. Grace stood up reminding Jen how hot her aunt was. Almost a head taller than Jen, Grace had to bend down to give her a hug. She wore tight brown leather pants, knee-high, lace-up boots, and a skin-tight black tee. When they released each other, both women said, "Wow."

Grace laughed and waved at the table's other chair. "You grew into an absolutely gorgeous young woman, little one."

Jen felt her cheeks get hot. "It's more of a curse than a blessing." She pointed to her size-too-large *Resident Evil* tee shirt. "Didn't dare wear anything nicer on the train."

Grace shrugged, "Yeah, I know." She handed over a red and white plastic menu. "But, no one'll hassle you here. Lunch's on me so don't deprive yourself."

Looking at the prices, Jen didn't figure Mary's would be one of her regular haunts while she was in school. She decided to accept Grace's offer to splurge. The waiter, a man Grace's age with full tattoo sleeves, industrials in his ears, and a lippy loop in the center of his bottom lip, disappeared after taking their orders.

Grace leaned forward and rested her square chin on her laced fingers. She kept her straight blond hair cut just below her ears and had four studs, in the rainbow colors, in each lobe. The enticing scent of leather wafted across the table. "There are things about me you don't know."

"I could say the same." Jen sipped from the pineapple juice that appeared at her elbow.

Grace laughed. "If you're going to tell me you're Lez, you needn't bother. I've known that since you were twelve." She took a swig from a bottle of Black Butte porter.

Jen choked on her juice and coughed repeatedly into her napkin. "How did you know?" She hadn't been aware of her own sexuality until high school when all the other girls were yammering about boys and she only wanted to hang with the girl's basketball squad.

"I've always been attracted to you, little one, your inquisitiveness, creativity, and oh the shenanigans..." She grinned. "You were part of my own coming to terms with my sexuality. Of course, I knew I needed to wait until you grew up. But, I remember being distinctly grateful we're not blood relations, especially since my mother's husband disowned me when I came out."

"I never forgave Dad's father for that. It pissed my folks off, though, when I refused to go to his funeral last year." Jen took a slower, smaller sip of the tangy sweet juice. "Anyway, I've always thought you're a total dykehot, but I don't understand why that means I can't stay with you?" Jen put on her flirtiest pout, pursing her full lips and batting her annoyingly long eyelashes over her baby blues.

Grace reached over and ran one finger along Jen's cheek, causing her to shiver. "That has nothing to do with it, you're legal now. But I just don't do vanilla and I'm not sure you're ready to be exposed to my lifestyle."

"I don't care. I need a place to live. If I have to find my own place, I'm destined to spend half my days on the Max, commuting in from Gresham. You live close enough for me to walk to school. I'm not asking for a handout. I can afford to pay some rent or do chores." Jen put one hand over her eyes and the other over her mouth. "I can be discreet, if you're worried about me telling anyone," she muttered from behind her hand.

The waiter set two loaded plates in front of them and Jen busied herself with cutting her burger in half.

"I don't need your discretion. I'm totally open. I'm concerned that living with me could negatively impact your standing in school, among your peers, when you look for a job..."

Jen looked up and watched Grace blow on a dark sweet potato fry before popping it into her mouth and couldn't help staring at the contours of her lips as she chewed. She wondered what they'd feel like on her... She shook her head. First she needed to convince Grace that she would make an acceptable roomie. Anything else could only be broached if it didn't jeopardize living together. "School policies prohibit harassment because of sexual orientation."

Grace took a huge bite from her Barbara-Q Bacon Burger and stared at Jen while she chewed, her greenish brown eyes tearing a hole in Jen's psyche. Jen dropped her eyes, picked up her own sandwich, and munched on an impressive combination of blue cheese, bacon, and succulent beef. When she swallowed, she looked up to see Grace still staring at her. "Okay, I know the harassment policies aren't worth the paper they're printed on, especially in a field with males outnumbering females ten to one. But, the school doesn't need to know where I live. I can get a P.O. box. My lifestyle's none of their business and I don't know why yours would be either."

"Do you even have a clue what I'm talking about, hun?"

Jen chewed another juicy bite. She could guess, but she didn't want to offend. "Leather?"

Grace laughed again and munched on her sandwich. "And, do you know what that means?"

Jen looked around at the surrounding tables, but everyone near them was engrossed in their own food and conversations. "Kinda hoping you might be willing to teach me. It's something I've been curious about for a while."

She looked up to find Grace staring at her, wide-eyed.

"I only look innocent." Jen extended her tongue and licked blue cheese dressing off the length of her finger.

Grace took a deep breath. "I don't live alone. I own a slave and I keep a sissy boy in a cage in the basement."

Jen blinked and pressed her lips together for a moment. "Hawt."

Grace laughed again and drained what was left in her bottle. "Maybe I'll take you home to meet my family. Then we can discuss potential living arrangements."

After a dude hit on Jen while they walked along Burnside, Grace took her hand and held it the rest of the way. The traffic on the busy street prevented conversation, so Jen had nothing to distract her from the heat radiating from Grace's fingers all the way to Jen's clit. She'd only had sex with two girls her own age and the results had been brief, awkward, and less than satisfying. The thought of an experienced older woman indulging her desire to explore something more adventurous made her crotch sticky.

They crossed over the freeway and turned north, the traffic noises dissipating as they entered the tree-lined streets near Couch Park. Grace unlocked the front door of her two-story duplex and Jen heard scurrying steps. A full-figured woman, wearing nothing but a steel ring around her neck, bounced down the stairs and prostrated herself in front of Grace, covering her boots with kisses. Her back and ass were crisscrossed with fading red welts. Grace smiled, then leaned down, grabbed a hank of the woman's long, dark, straight hair, not unlike Jen's own, and brought her head up so she looked at Jen.

"Jen, this is my slave, Emma. Gurl, this is my," Grace cleared her throat, "niece, Jen." Grace released the woman's hair and she nodded her head in Jen's direction.

"Most pleased to make your acquaintance, Miss." She had a black rose tattooed on her right breast, and a colorful half sleeve of thorns, snakes, and other symbols from her shoulder to her left elbow. She unlaced Grace's boots, set them on a mat under the coat rack and replaced them with leather slippers, kissing Grace's feet in between each step.

Jen slid her backpack off her shoulders, relieved to be free of the weight, and set it up against the wall next to the front door.

"May I assist you with your shoes, Miss?" Emma held up a pair of black, terrycloth mules.

"No, I can, thanks, that's okay." Jen felt herself blushing. She kicked off her Lo-Tops in the general direction of the mat and stuck her feet in the slippers.

Emma leaned over and lined up Jen's sneakers with the mat.

"Come on, I'll show you what your options are if I decide this is workable." Grace strode into the granite and stainless kitchen, through a door, and down a set of plain wooden stairs. The huge room, paneled in dark pine, was divided in half by a wall of steel bars. A small gate near the far end was secured with a five-inch padlock. The side they stood on only had a worn, black suede sofa against one windowless wall. The scent of bleach and laundry soap emanated from a partially open door at the far end.

On the other side of the bars, someone wearing black taffeta trimmed in white lace knelt on the carpeted floor, chest on knees, arms stretched out pointing toward Grace. That half of the room had a computer desk with a large monitor, a thin mattress on the floor, an ironing board, and a garment rack with a dozen black dresses hanging from it. A toilet, sink, and enclosed shower stall occupied a corner. The only demarcation between the "bathroom" and the rest of the area was vinyl floor instead of blood red carpet.

Grace pointed to the prostrate figure. "This is Sissy. We could string a curtain across the bars and set up a bedroom for you here. It's not exactly private, though, and you'd have to come upstairs to use the bathroom."

Before Jen could respond, Grace spun on her heel and returned to the kitchen. Jen followed her up a polished mahogany staircase to the second floor. Grace walked past open double doors at the top of the stairs and Jen caught a glimpse of a king bed with an antique brass headboard, a leather recliner, a tall armoire and wide dresser, both of dark wood. Everything was massive and gleamed in the dim light filtering through tall windows.

Grace opened a door down the hall from the bedroom. "This is my office. You'd have to be out of here when I'm working, usually between ten in the morning and eight in the evening, sometimes earlier, sometimes later, depending on deadlines."

Floor to ceiling walnut bookcases filled with paperback computer manuals, a hard bound Lovecraft collection, and an impressive stash of role-playing books, covered one wall of the room. A huge walnut desk with three flat-screen monitors and a pull-out keyboard tray sat in front of the window. Along the far wall, a black leather sofa stood next to a small closed door.

"The sofa opens up into a bed and I can empty out that closet for you." Grace left and Jen followed her down the hall to another closed door. When Grace ushered her inside, Jen just stood there her eyes wide, her mouth open. A massage table stood against one wall, and a sturdy, polished wooden rack of foot-wide, open squares filled the opposite corner. Floggers, whips, cuff sets, and many items Jen couldn't identify hung on one wall. A dresser and open shelves on the window wall held more interesting looking pieces, and there were giant hooks in the ceiling.

"I could set you up in here with a blow up bed. Again, I can empty the closet and probably a drawer or two. I don't get in here nearly as often as I'd like, maybe once or twice a week. So it wouldn't be your space either, but you'd have more privacy in here than in my office or the basement." Grace stood with her arms crossed under her pert breasts, watching Jen. "Unless, of course any of this squicks you out."

"I'd have to say whichever is less inconvenient for you. It's going to take me at least two years, possibly three to earn my game art design degree. Can you put up with me that long?"

Grace laughed. "If you stay out of my hair, sure. You'll have to share a bathroom with Emma and get along with her as well, of course. It doesn't matter if Sissy likes you or not, in fact, you're welcome to take out any frustrations that build up dealing with the nerds at school on her." Grace backed up to the massage table and boosted herself up to sit on it, swinging her long legs. "It'd be better if you could afford your own place, but as long as I don't have to adjust my lifestyle, you're welcome to stay until you get a job."

"Thanks so much, Aunt Grace." Jen dropped to her knees and mimicked Emma's action, kissing the top of one slipper and then the other, the leather smooth against her lips, the smell of polish mingling with the scent of tanning chemicals.

Grace reached down and ran her fingers through Jen's long, black hair, tightening them at Jen's neck and pulling her up between her knees. "Well, now, if you behave like that, you'll be more than welcome here." She pressed her mouth against Jen's and Jen wrapped her arms around Grace's waist.

Holding Jen's hair with one hand, Grace stroked her cheek with the other. Jen melted into her arms, her lips trembling, her knees turning to rubber.

"You sure? I don' t do vanilla."

"Please?" Jen couldn't catch her breath. Her heart was thumping in her ears.

"Do you like pain?"

Jen shrugged her shoulders.

"Bondage?"

Jen shrugged again.

"Do you have a clue what you do like?"

Jen shook her head.

"But, you want to explore?"

Jen managed to move her head up and down an inch.

Grace kissed her and pulled Jen's lower lip into her mouth. She pressed her teeth against the tender flesh, gently at first, then harder until Jen squeaked. Grace chuckled, but she was breathing hard as well. In the distance, Jen heard the jangle of a ringtone, but her world had narrowed to Grace's teeth on her lips, the taste of porter mingled with barbecue sauce, small firm breasts pressed against hers, strong arms wrapped around her shoulders, and the smell of leather.

When Grace released her lip, Jen felt dizzy and disoriented. She leaned against her aunt. Grace pulled her up onto the table so they were sitting side-by-side and held her. "We really should talk before we go any further."

"Please. Don't stop." Jen had no idea what Grace would do, but she didn't care. She didn't want the euphoric sensations to end. Her clit throbbed with need.

Grace gripped her chin in her fingers. "Look at me, little one."

Jen blinked and met her aunt's piercing stare.

"You don't understand what you're getting into. I'm going to go slow and I'm going to expect you to stay with me enough to be able to tell me if it gets to be too much. Can you do that?"

Jen managed to keep her eyes open long enough to nod. "Yes, Ma'am," she whispered.

Grace chuckled and kissed her on the forehead. "You can't imagine how long I've wished I could do this."

Jen just smiled. Grace slipped off the table and pulled Jen's tee shirt over her head, unclasped her bra, and palmed one breast while sucking on the other nipple. Her fingers pinched Jen's right nipple as her teeth clamped down on the left. Gradually the pressure increased and Jen moaned, pushing her chest forward toward her tormentor's hand and mouth. Grace laughed, but released Jen's tits. She whimpered.

"Don't worry, little one. I'm not going to neglect these pretties. Just want to make you more comfortable." She guided Jen's shoulders down to a prone position and unzipped her jeans, sliding pants and panties off together. "After you hang these up, give me the clip box."

Jen blinked rapidly and turned to see Emma's ample rear as she draped her jeans on a hook on the back of the door, next to the one holding Jen's shirt and undies. The woman handed Grace a box and her huge tits came so very close, Jen couldn't resist reaching up to stroke them. She saw Emma and Grace exchange looks and then the younger woman moved closer so her big brown nipple dangled right above Jen's mouth.

Jen stuck out her tongue and tweaked the succulent nub. Emma lowered her breast and Jen drew the nipple into her mouth. Something pinched her own nipple. It stung briefly and then tingled deliciously all the way down to her clit. Jen bit Emma's nipple. The woman groaned and Jen smelled her arousal mingling with the scent of her own and Grace's. The combined aroma, mixed with leather from the massage table and Grace's pants, was heavenly. Another sharp pain and then another erupted along her right breast.

Jen lifted her hands to clasp the wonderful tit in her mouth and Emma stroked her hair. She was grateful Grace had laid her down. She'd never have kept her feet with this much sensation bombarding her. More pinches marched down her sides and gradually gripped the inside of both thighs. She opened her legs as wide as she could on the narrow table, hoping that would tempt Grace to explore her folds. She was dripping now, juices pooling under her ass. Jen lifted her hips up from the table, but Grace slapped her mound.

"I get to decide when I'm ready to play with that."

Jen removed her mouth from Emma's nipple long enough to whisper, "Yes, Ma'am." Emma took advantage and shifted so when Jen closed her lips again, it was on a completely dry nipple, not yet hardened. Jen got to work addressing that deficit, sucking, tonguing, and biting. Her hands wandered from Emma's tits along her curves and folds seeking her ass. Emma guided her fingers until she could grip the plump cheeks and caress the welts.

Jen heard buzzing and opened her eyes. Grace held up a large, purple, vibrating dildo, her head tilted to one side. Jen nodded. Grace guided the toy to Jen's lips, teasing her, barely making contact with her flesh. Jen lifted her hips again, and Grace slapped her down. Jen cried out as much from need as pain.

Grace removed one of the clips pinching her tit and Jen

howled. Grace removed another as she guided the dildo between Jen's lips, its vibrations hovering just outside her cunt. So close. If Jen lifted her hips, she'd make contact, but Grace would only pull it away to slap her. Emma widened her stance and guided Jen's left hand along her hip to her hairless mound. Jen dipped one finger in the moistness and brought it back to her mouth, sucking off the honey. Grace removed the clips from her breasts. Each one hurt more than the next, as blood flowed back into her pinched flesh.

Jen thrust two fingers deeper into Emma's dripping cunt. With her thumb, she massaged Emma's clit and toyed with the ring piercing her hood. Jen gasped when the dildo finally penetrated her quim and she shook all over as the orgasm exploded outward. Emma's cunt clenched down on Jen's fingers. Her curves jiggled and both hands gripped the massage table. She leaned over and kissed Jen, her tongue stroking the tender spot where Grace had bitten Jen's lip.

Grace ran her hands lightly over Jen's bruised legs and tits. Jen floated in post-orgasmic euphoria. Ecstasy enveloped her entire body, making it impossible to move, and swaddled her brain in a soft, pink haze. She'd never had an experience like this before and promised herself she would do anything Grace asked to enjoy more like it.

Jen let herself into the duplex and kicked her shoes at the wall with a satisfying thunk. She was so tired of the abuse. Despite fake glasses, keeping her hair in a tight ponytail, avoiding makeup and nail polish, wearing only baggy jeans and tee shirts, and adorning herself with every piece of Pride jewelry she could find, each and every one of her classmates had hit on her in the first three weeks of school. Half of them reacted to her announcement that she was a Lesbian with either hostility or disbelief accompanied by an implied threat to prove she just hadn't met the "right" man. She was the only woman in two of her three classes and the other female student was forty pounds overweight with greasy hair, pimples, and coke bottle glasses that she really needed.

Apparently most women in the game design program had dropped out or switched majors before their third year. To save money, Jen had taken most of the required drawing, figure studies, modeling, texturing, and lighting classes at University of Oregon. Now she wondered if she would have been better off staying in Eugene and getting a graphics design certificate at Lane County Community College.

But then, she wouldn't be living in heaven with Grace and Emma. Maybe she'd just transfer to Portland State.

"What's wrong little one?" Grace stood at the top of the stairs red hot in black jeans and tee.

"Same old, same old."

"Gamer turds?"

Jen nodded. "Yes, Ma'am."

"How much homework do you have?"

"I've got two big projects due Monday, but nothing tomorrow."

Grace whistled and Emma emerged from the kitchen, wiping her hands on a dish towel. "Yes, Mistress?"

"Go get Sissy."

"Yes, Mistress."

"Come on up, hun. I can't help you with the scum at school, but I can provide you with an outlet for your frustration."

Jen dropped her backpack off in the corner of the living room where Grace had set up a small desk for her computer and headed upstairs to the playroom. Emma arrived a few minutes later leading Sissy by a chain attached to the steel collar around Sissy's neck. She wore one of her ubiquitous crisp black taffeta dresses with white lace at collar, sleeves and waist, three-inch heels, and black stockings.

Sissy dropped to her knees in front of Grace. "Goddess, if you would indulge me. Before you turn me over to the beautiful young Miss, may I offer her a few words of advice?"

Grace nodded and Sissy turned on her knees to face Jen. "Beautiful Miss, before I came to serve here, I worked at Electronic Arts. It's possible, if extremely difficult, for a woman to succeed in game design. May I make a few suggestions?"

Jen nodded.

"If I may be so bold, you'll do better if you were girly without being too feminine. Ditch the glasses. Guys can tell they're not real, even if it's just subconsciously, then they have no reason to believe you when tell them you're Gay. Be friendly to your classmates, even the ones who've hit on you. Friendly, like a 'bro,' " she held her immaculately manicured fingers up in quote marks, "not like a potential date. You have to remember, these guys could be the ones you're working with or for when you graduate. You need to start making connections now, especially since you're coming in late to the game." She snickered at her own joke, then hung her head. "I'm sorry, I know this is serious, I know you've put up with a lot of abuse. But if you don't try to fit in and make connections now, you'll never find work in the field once you graduate. It's not fair, but women get held to higher standards. They're expected to be easy on eyes, but still know what they're doing and be good at it."

Sissy fell to her chest on the floor. "Please forgive me. I'd help you if I could, but I'm afraid I burned all those bridges when I disappeared into the Goddess's dungeon."

Jen swallowed. Sissy's suggestions sounded just as bad as hiding behind baggy clothes, fake glasses, and no makeup. "Thanks, Sissy. I'll try."

"Strip." Grace looked at Emma who unhooked the leash.

"Yes, Goddess, thank you, Goddess." Sissy lifted her skirts over her head and pulled off her dress. Underneath she wore only a black garter belt holding up her stockings. Inchwide rings hung from both her nipples and she had a Prince Albert piercing in her cock.

Grace crossed her arms. "Gurl, string him up." She nodded toward the wall of toys. "Jen, what would you like to use to vent your frustration with your dickwad classmates?" Her evil grin sent a shiver down Jen's spine.

Emma locked leather cuffs to Sissy's wrists and stood on a stool. She pulled Sissy's arms above her head and attached the cuffs to one of the ceiling hooks. Climbing down, she pushed Sissy's legs apart and fastened another set of cuffs, separated by a three-foot long steel bar, to her ankles.

"What can I hit her, errr him with?" Grace had never referred to Sissy using the male pronoun before. But, then Jen had never seen him naked, either.

"How about these?" Grace held out two leather paddles. She lifted the one that was eighteen inches long and six inches wide, first. "Use this one to hit his ass, thighs, upper arms, and shoulders." She raised the other, only six inches by one inch. "And this one is for his cock."

Jen grinned and took the smaller one. Sissy smiled at her, his cock sticking straight out. She tapped him between the metal ring protruding from his pee hole and his shaved pelvis.

"Thank you, Beautiful Miss. May I have another?"

"You can hit him a lot harder than that, hun," Grace said.

Jen drew her arm back and whacked him again, this time getting a lovely slapping sound and causing his cock to bounce.

"Thank you, Beautiful Miss. May I have another?" His voice was pitched just a bit higher.

Jen snickered and hit him again.

"Thank you, Beautiful Miss. May I have another?"

She hit him five times in a row, and he repeated "Thank you, Beautiful Miss. May I have another?" five times.

Jen had to admit that hitting a cock did make her feel better. She let loose another barrage.

"Thank you, Miss Beautiful. May I have another?" he squeaked.

Jen tilted her head, noting the reordering of his nickname for her.

"You'll have to switch to the bigger paddle for a bit." Grace handed it to her and took the little one. "That's all the little wuss can handle on his cock."

"I'm so sorry, Goddess." Sissy hung his head and looked like he might cry. "I'll try to take more."

Jen stepped behind him and rubbed the paddle against the globes of Sissy's ass the way Grace had taught her. She hauled back and swung it hard, landing it across both his cheeks, leaving a lovely red mark and throwing him off balance.

He regained his footing. "Thank you, Beautiful Miss. May I have another?"

Jen swung again, producing a satisfying thwack.

"Thank you, Beautiful Miss. May I have another?"

She swung again and again, hitting his ass and the tops of his thighs until her arms ached.

"Thank you, Beautiful Miss. May I have another?"

Grace took the paddle. "I'm afraid not, she's worn herself out." She gathered Jen into her arms and kissed her.

Jen was surprised by her own arousal.

Emma came up behind her and pressed her immense breasts into her back. "Feel better, Sweetie?"

Grace's tongue filled her mouth, and Jen could only let out a moan deep in her throat that emerged sounding like a cat's purr. Emma pulled out the elastic tie from Jen's hair, let it spill down her back, and ran her fingers through it. Jen watched Sissy sway from side-to-side, turning around in his bonds so he faced them. He stared brazenly at the three of them as Emma undressed her.

Jen reluctantly pulled her head back from Grace's lips. "He's watching."

Grace laughed. "That's his reward, his only reward, for being a good boy and letting you beat him."

Jen tilted her head. "He's not a masochist?"

Grace stepped back so Emma could finish stripping off Jen's clothing. "Not really, more of a pain slut. He doesn't get off on the pain itself so much as pleasing the one who's hurting him."

Jen shrugged. She wasn't sure about Sissy watching her have sex, but he certainly had been with Grace much longer than she and it wasn't her place to question the household dynamics. Emma was caressing her breasts from behind, pinching her nipples, and Jen found it surprisingly easy to forget about Sissy hanging at the far end of the room.

Emma and Jen jumped at the crack of Grace's whip over their heads. They turned to face each other and their mouths clamped together. Jen felt the first lash across her ass as Emma's tongue pushed between her lips. She kept her arms tight around the woman's neck, knowing Grace expected her to stay upright, but not sure she could.

She heard the next stroke, but felt nothing. From the delectable musk reaching her nostrils, she assumed Emma had been the recipient. Grace alternated between them, although sometimes she startled Jen by hitting her twice in a row. Jen could feel welts building up on her ass and shoulders, but didn't dare stroke the ones on Emma's backs for fear of catching the whip on her hands. They kept their mouths locked together, their tongues trading places when the whip did.

Jen lost her footing and Emma had to hold her up. Grace grabbed her and the two women carried her to the bedroom. They left her lying on her stomach, the red satin comforter cool against her heated skin, while Emma undressed Grace. Jen would have liked to watch, but she was too stoned on endorphins to open her eyes. The mattress sank on either side of her as they joined her in the bed. Emma's meaty hands and Grace's long, slender fingers stroked the welts along her ass and back. Jen wiggled, and Emma kissed her rear.

They eased her onto her back. Grace knelt over her face and Jen stuck out her tongue eagerly. The older woman teased her, only getting low enough for Jen's tongue to barely reach her blond bush. Jen felt Emma's kisses on the inside of her thighs and moaned. Finally Grace lowered herself so Jen could lap at the French vanilla ambrosia that dripped onto her face. She forced herself to raise her head off the bed so she could bury her mouth in Grace's luscious cunt and find her clit.

Emma had worked her nose in between Jen's lips and she heard her inhale before her tongue emerged to lick up Jen's own juices. Jen managed to get her foot between Emma's plump thighs and jiggled her hood ring with her toe. Emma sighed into her cunt and Jen pushed her hips up toward the sound. She found it hard to remember to lick and toe fuck while Emma's talented tongue nudged her clit, but Grace moaned and Emma made a purring sound deep in her throat. Jen held onto Grace's wondrously tight ass cheeks while Emma squirmed on her toe.

Grace came first, gushing all over Jen's face. That meant she and Emma had permission to come and Emma grabbed Jen's clit in her teeth and prodded it with her tongue until Jen's entire body shook and her pussy spasmed over and over again. When Grace lay down next to Jen, stroking her arm, Emma turned around and positioned her crotch in front of Jen's face. Jen dove in, licking the honey nectar, pushing her tongue into Emma's cunt, and teasing her clit. When Emma grabbed Jen's head, she clamped down on her clit and sucked on it until Emma came, hard.

"Feel better?" Grace whispered in her ear.

Jen managed to nod. Emma rolled off the bed and Jen opened her eyes, noting that Sissy knelt in the corner, his cock still sticking straight out. Emma turned around and lay back down facing Jen. Although hyper aware of the firm tits behind her and the luscious mounds in front of her, Jen floated unaware of her own physical form.

One term, she decided. She'd try to follow Sissy's advice and give the Art Institute one full term. If she couldn't make at least two friends by the end of the year, she was transferring to another program. But, first she'd give it her best shot.

Leather Family

By I.G. Frederick

"Ma'am?" Kyle knelt to one side of the easy chair.

"Yes, boy." Monica set her newspaper on her lap and looked at the 47-year-old, six foot three, 230-pound Kyle.

"I've met a guy. I really like him. I was wondering..." He lowered his eyes. Not the reaction Monica would have expected under the circumstances.

"Tell me about him." She removed her reading glasses and rested them on top of her head.

"Met him last week at the board meeting. He's 38, with red hair, green eyes, and all the fire of an Irish boy, but his family's from France. Motorcycle mechanic, good one too, from what I've learned."

Monica raised one eyebrow. "You've checked him out?"

"Well, Ma'am, it'd be irresponsible for me to take an interest in someone you found unsuitable."

Monica smiled. She couldn't fault Kyle's approach. Couldn't fault him for much; he'd served her well for nearly six years now.

19

"Jacques, spelled with a q, served as a slave in a leather family in Chicago. He couldn't hack the winters there any more and was released to move back here about six months ago."

"Sounds lovely, what's the catch?"

Kyle looked surprised for maybe a nanosecond.

We know each other too well, Monica said to herself and smiled.

"He's gay."

Monica laughed. And laughed. Tears formed at the corners of her eyes. Kyle sat back on his heels, rested his hands palms up on his thighs, and lowered his chin to his chest. Monica put one finger under each eye to catch the moisture and pondered the dilemma her slave had presented.

On the one hand, she had always wanted another boy in the family. Kyle and Lisbet served her well and she loved them both dearly. But like her, Kyle was bisexual. He needed a male in his life, and the switch in him would benefit from his own toy to abuse.

Monica adored watching two men together -- it was her favourite type of porn. She had a long list of fantasies that involved two men and herself. But, she frowned, her fantasies wouldn't work if one of those men was gay. Still, she certainly didn't need any more sex herself; Kyle and Lisbet met all her needs in that regard. Finding someone who would fit into her leather family outweighed sexuality concerns. She wondered if a gay boy would even consider serving in a house that included two women, and how Lisbet would react.

Reaching over, Monica touched Kyle's chin. He brought his piercing blue eyes up to stare into hers, questions putting a crease between his eyebrows.

"You may court him. You know what I require in terms of testing before you bring him home. He has to understand that I will own him and he will serve me as well as you. You may promise him that he will only have sexual interactions with you." If the ownership issue did not prove to be a deal breaker, Monica figured her last condition would. "However, he also must agree that I get to watch those interactions whenever I want and that he will be required to have sex with you while you're having sex with me."

The smile started with a wicked glint in Kyle's eyes and spread to his lips which pushed in the dimples on his cheeks. "Yes, Ma'am. Thank you, Ma'am."

$\mathcal{M}$

Six weeks later, Kyle brought Jacques home to meet the family. After each date, Kyle had had with the boy, he became more and more enthusiastic about bringing Jacques into the house. He praised the boy's obedience and exuberance and Monica could see that he was smitten. Although surprised the boy would agree to her conditions, she looked forward to meeting someone her slave could find that appealing.

The smell of chicken and tomatoes simmering in the kitchen permeated the living room. Monica had dressed up a little for the occasion, forgoing her usual shorts and tank top for a straight, knee-length black skirt and a silky black blouse. But the boys arrived earlier than expected. When Monica heard the door to the carport open, Lisbet had her pretty blonde head between Monica's legs and Monica was too close to coming to pull her out from under her skirt.

While Lisbet ran her very talented tongue up and down Monica's slit, probing deep into Monica's pussy and tickling her clit, Monica watched the boys stripping in the entry. Kyle walked into the living room and assumed the position near Monica's feet. Jacques followed, putting one hand across his chest, the other behind his back and bowing from the waist until his forehead almost reached the floor.

With two handsome naked boys in front of her and the view of Lisbet's bare arse still red from the paddling she had enjoyed earlier, Monica shook with orgasm. She refrained from crying out, instead gripping the arms of the chair as the spasms travelled from Lisbet's tongue through Monica's entire body. When Lisbet had sucked up all the come, Monica grabbed her hair and kissed her forehead. "Go finish preparing dinner, my pretty."

"Yes, Ma'am; thank you, Ma'am." Lisbet touched her lips to each of Monica's feet in turn and backed out of the room, her lovely breasts jiggling as she reached up to tie back her hair before returning to the kitchen.

"Master Monica, may I present slave candidate Jacques?" Kyle said, nodding to first her and then to the new boy.

In one fluid, sensual movement, Jacques, who had stayed in his bow while Monica finished with Lisbet, dropped to his knees and put his head between them, his chest resting on his thighs. "I am most honoured to make your acquaintance, Ma'am. Sir Kyle has explained to me the terms of your household." His voice was flat and his words sounded rehearsed. "I would like to humbly beg for permission to petition you for the opportunity to be taken into consideration for your collar." He raised himself from the floor, without using his hands, and sat back on his heels, his hands on his thighs his eyes downward.

Monica frowned. "I'll hear your petition now." She wondered if he had prepared for that possibility.

He stole a glance at Kyle, but spoke after hesitating only a moment. "Thank you so much for the privilege, Ma'am. I served for six years in the House of Grey Panther, an all-male leather family in Chicago. Master Panther had four boys in service to him; I was the most recent acquisition. I primarily served Master Panther's alpha, who was the house major domo, as personal BDSM toy and sex slave. I also took care of all of the family vehicles. The beta boy was a stay-at-home housekeeper and cook, the rest of us all had outside jobs."

The boy paused for a moment. When Monica asked no questions, he continued. "A couple of years ago, I started having serious bouts of bronchitis and I ended up in the hospital more than once. I'd moved from Carson City to Chicago to serve Master Panther, and my doctor highly recommended that I move back for my health. I wanted to stay in service; I was willing to fly back monthly. But Master Panther only accepts boys who can live with him full time."

Jacques blinked his eyes rapidly for a moment and swallowed. "When I came back here, I got a job as a motorcycle mechanic and rented a room over the shop until I could find a new family. I joined Friends of Leather when I first arrived, but only started going to board meetings a couple of months ago. I pretty much attend any leather event I find out about, trying to meet someone I can serve." He frowned. "I'm not sure what else you might like to know, Ma'am."

Lisbet stepped back into the living room and knelt at Monica's feet, placing herself just slightly behind Kyle, but making sure she was closer than Jacques. "Ma'am, dinner is ready whenever you are. If you could let me know when you'd like me to serve, I'd be most grateful."

Monica smiled. "What do you think about having another male in the house?"

Lisbet shrugged her shoulders and her long, blonde hair tumbled across the luscious mounds of her breasts. "Whatever pleases Ma'am, makes me happy." Lisbet frowned and Monica recognised that she did not like the idea at all. "I am glad he's gay, though." Her green eyes wandered toward the metal tube encasing Kyle's cock. "Not that I think Kyle would ever, I mean..." She blushed, the rosy colour spreading from her cheeks, down her long, slender neck, to her chest.

"We'd make quite the family, wouldn't we, covering the full spectrum: one lesbian, one gay boy, and a bisexual of either gender." Monica decided to ignore Lisbet's concern for the moment. She had not yet decided whether Jacques was even suitable. "Go ahead and serve dinner, Lisbet. We can continue this conversation at the table."

Lisbet scurried back to the kitchen and Monica rose and walked to the dining room, the two boys behind her. Kyle pulled out the padded arm chair for her, then took his place behind one of the three, plain wooden chairs surrounding the round oak table. He pointed to the one next to him, but Jacques stayed behind Kyle. When Monica nodded, giving Kyle permission to sit, Jacques pulled out the chair and then went to stand behind the one Kyle had indicated.

This could get interesting, Monica thought. Although Kyle was her alpha, Lisbet only served Monica and the two worked as a team to make sure Monica's needs were met. If she added Jacques to the family, although his auto-mechanic skills would come in handy, he would mostly serve Kyle.

Lisbet brought out a white soup tureen and set it on a trivet on one side of Monica's plate. She returned to the kitchen and came back with a steaming bowl of rice in one hand and green beans in the other. After spooning rice onto Monica's plate, Lisbet lifted the lid of the tureen, releasing the aroma of cardamom and cloves. She topped the rice with the tomato and chicken mixture and added green beans to the far side of the plate, careful to keep them from the spreading tomato sauce.

When Monica picked up her fork, Lisbet stood behind the last chair. Monica blew on the chicken-rice concoction before savouring the spicy flavours. Then she nodded to all three in turn. Lisbet and Jacques took their seats and Kyle helped himself to the food, passing each dish to Lisbet who handed them to Jacques after filling her own plate. When they all had served themselves, Monica raised her wine glass. "To growing families." She sipped the light Riesling. Lisbet and Kyle did the same, but Jacques only drank from his water glass.

"You don't drink?"

"No, Ma'am. Got into a bit of trouble when I was young and I found it best if I stay away from alcohol."

Monica frowned, wondering how long ago he had conquered the problem and whether she would have to worry what might cause him to have a relapse. "Did Master Panther keep you in chastity?"

Jacques, set down his fork full of food. "Yes, Ma'am. Although he used a different type of device than the one Sir Kyle wears. Brian, his alpha, had the key." He lifted the fork and stuffed it in his mouth as if afraid Monica's questions would keep him from eating. When he swallowed, he said. "Wow, Ma'am. Miss here's quite a good cook."

Lisbet straightened her shoulders and her smile made her eyes sparkle. "Thank you, Jacques. Ma'am has been good enough to allow me to take cooking classes on occasion."

Jacques praise of Lisbet's cooking would help win the girl over, Monica, thought. Lisbet took great pride in her culinary skills. Still, Monica questioned the wisdom of bringing a gay boy into the family. "Did your Master mark you?" Monica took another sip of the wine, letting the crisp fruit bathe away the spice of the chicken before she tasted the delicate green beans.

"No, Ma'am. I've had these tattoos ..." he pointed to the tribal on his well-developed right bicep and the Celtic knot on his left "... since my drinking days, Ma'am."

Monica looked at both of them from across the table. "At least you had good taste even when intoxicated. Are you prepared to wear my mark if I accept you in my house and honour you with my collar?"

Both Kyle and Lisbet had Monica's initials tattooed on their left breasts. Kyle also had a dragon that covered most of his back and Lisbet a rose on a thorny stem at the base of her spine.

"Ma'am, I've known the joy of enslavement and the terror of living on my own again. I find Sir Kyle very attractive, intelligent, and knowledgeable. I would like very much to serve him. I haven't met anyone in the leatherman scene here who appealed to me in any way. That's one of the reasons I ended up in Chicago in the first place. If I must wear your mark to gain admittance to this house, I can accept that."

Monica nodded to Kyle to take over the conversational lead, allowing him to turn to more general topics for the rest of the meal. But, she paid little attention to the discourse.

Jacques' comment that he would wear her mark if he must, worried her. She feared that in his desire to serve Kyle, Jacques would promise to accept conditions that he would eventually find insufferable.

A comment from Lisbet drew Monica back into the conversation. "Yes, I'd prefer to serve a lesbian, but we can't help who we fall in love with." She shrugged. "And, let's face it, the opportunities here are limited. I work for the state and don't have the option of moving to a bigger city to find the perfect family."

Jacques gave her a half smile. "May I ask how long you've served Master Monica?"

"Four years as of November." Lisbet looked up and smiled when she saw Monica watching her. "The family situation may not be perfect, but I can't imagine serving anyone else. And truth be told, I like Kyle. He's become the older brother I never had."

After they enjoyed Lisbet's chocolate cake, Monica returned to the living room followed by Lisbet and Jacques. While Kyle cleared the table and washed the dishes, Lisbet massaged Monica's feet. Jacques knelt in the centre of the room.

"Are you a masochist, boy?"

"Brian says I'm more of a pain slut, Ma'am. He would beat me until he broke skin, do CBT for hours, and leave me bound and caged, sometimes overnight."

Monica looked between Jacques' muscled legs and licked her lips. Even flaccid, his cock almost touched the floor. "I'm rather fond of cock and ball torture myself. How do you feel about me doing that to you?" He *would* make an attractive addition to her family, despite his sexuality.

Jacques winced. "Ma'am, if you are the one who owns me, I would expect you could do whatever you wish to me." He swallowed several times, his Adam's apple bouncing up and down in his neck. "The only thing I don't think I could manage, Ma'am ..." He closed his eyes. "I mean would I be required… may I ask that I not have to do anything involving umm, girl parts, Ma'am?"

Lisbet smothered a snicker by taking Monica's big toe in her mouth and Monica had to repress a laugh.

"You can say pussy, boy. We all know what it is. To clarify, you wouldn't complain if I beat you or abused your prick, but you're asking me not to make you stick your face or your cock in my pussy or anyone else's?"

Jacques let out all the air in his lungs and gasped it in again. "Yes, Ma'am. Thank you for understanding, Ma'am." His face had gone from pale to pink to fire engine red.

"And Kyle explained to you the rules, requirements, and protocols of my house?"

"Yes, Ma'am. Not too much different than what Master Panther required. Is that why you go by Master instead of Mistress, Ma'am?"

Monica laughed. "No, I go by Master because I'm not a kept woman or someone's illicit love affair. I am the master of this house, this family."

"Thank you, Ma'am. I apologise for my presumption, Ma'am."

"Never apologise for asking questions, boy. How are you going to learn otherwise?"

"Yes, Ma'am. Thank you, Ma'am."

"How were you used sexually in the Grey Panther house?"

"I serviced all the others orally and Brian, mostly, but Master Panther occasionally ..." he blushed again then raised his eyebrows and whispered, "... fucked me in the arse."

"Have *you* ever fucked anyone in the arse, boy?" Just the thought of Kyle's face between her legs while another man buggered him made Monica wet.

"No, Ma'am. I'm sorry, I'm not sure I could do that. I've always been a bottom sexually, even before I got involved in the BDSM scene." Jacques shoulders sagged.

Monica scowled. She should have known a boy who had spent six years at the low end of the hierarchy in a gay male household wouldn't be able to top her boy. Kyle had never submitted to a male and had been served by both men and women over the years before she met him and captured his heart.

She looked at the crestfallen face of the boy kneeling in front of her. He *was* cute, and he did have a good background. She could understand why Kyle found him attractive. But even after revising all her fantasy scenarios to include a gay male, they still wouldn't work if the one who bottomed was also the one who disliked pussy.

For a few moments, she lost herself in Lisbet's skilful ministrations to her feet.

"May I speak, Ma'am?"

"Yes, boy."

"I'm sorry, Ma'am. I understand you would prefer a bisexual boy. Frankly, I wish I could find a family more like the one I had in Chicago. But, the reality is, the man I very much want to serve finds you worthy of his worship. And given the choice between living alone and joining a family that includes women, I think I would prefer the latter. I do have three sisters, Ma'am, so I'm not completely unfamiliar with the differences of a house that's all male versus one that includes ladies."

Monica didn't open her eyes, enjoying Lisbet's firm thumbs manipulating the muscles on her heel while she pondered the possibilities.

"I would very much appreciate the opportunity to see if I can fit into your household."

Monica took a deep breath and pressed the upper button on the remote she wore on a chain around her neck. Would have to get another one of these.

"Yes, Ma'am." Kyle knelt in front of her, drying his hands on a dish towel. The slightly pained, slightly shocked look he got when she zapped the electronic dog collar wrapped around his balls slowly fading. "Would you like some tea, Ma'am?"

"No, Kyle." She lifted the chain over her head and picked

out one of the keys. "I want to see what this boy can do."

Kyle handed the dish towel to Jacques and stood in front of Monica with his hands on the back of his neck, his elbows facing outward. Monica unlocked the small padlock and Kyle stepped back to remove the pieces that attached the tube to his cock by means of his frenum piercing. He set them, along with the dog collar, on the coffee table. Although Jacques still kept his head pointed downward, his own cock got hard when Kyle's was released and immediately became erect. Monica eyed them both with appreciation for their physique and their endowments.

"You may leave, Lisbet. Finish up whatever still needs doing in the kitchen and then you may have computer time."

"Thank you very much, Ma'am." Lisbet kissed each of Monica's feet and walked away, snatching the dish towel from Jacques.

Monica snapped her fingers at Kyle and pointed to her lap. He knelt in front of her, placed her feet on his shoulders, and slowly kissed his way up her inner thighs.

"There's the man you wish to serve, boy," Monica said to Jacques. "You figure out how to worship him."

"Yes, Ma'am." Jacques' voice had deepened considerably. "Thank you, Ma'am."

He scooched around to one side and peered at the very small gap between Kyle's knees and Monica's and frowned for a moment. Then he licked his lips, crawled behind Kyle, lay on his back, and inched himself between Kyle's legs until he could lick Kyle's shaved balls. Kyle had worked his way up to Monica's nether lips and he moaned when Jacques' tongue caressed his sack. The sound hit Monica's wet nub just as Kyle's tongue found it and she sighed with pleasure. She spread her legs, draping them over the arms of the chair, so if she leaned to one side she could watch when Jacques raised his head and wrapped his lips around Kyle's pierced cock. Kyle lapped up Monica's juices and bathed her clit in slick warmth.

Despite the awkwardness of the two men trying not to

interfere with each other's movements, the bliss of watching Jacques' head bob up and down while he sucked Kyle's cock and Kyle's tongue lavishing attention on her clit sent Monica over the edge. She moaned and gushed. While Kyle worked hard to capture all her juices, Monica thought of another possibility.

She grabbed Kyle's hair and pulled his head away. His eyes had a gleam that said he wasn't all there so she dropped her feet from Kyle's shoulders to Jacques', forcing the boy to release Kyle's cock. When she had Kyle's attention, she said, "Condoms, lube, and the chair."

Kyle shook his head to clear it. "Yes, Ma'am." He struggled to his feet and tore out of the room, leaving Jacques lying at the foot of Monica's chair. Moments later Kyle returned with condoms in one hand, a bottle of lube in the other, and the arm of Monica's queening chair hanging over his elbow. He set that on the floor and positioned himself on his back with his face under the hole in the middle of the leather seat.

Monica moved to the short-legged chair and Kyle immediately went back to work. She pointed at the condoms and lube still in his hands and his cock, which stood straight up, and looked at Jacques. "You should be able to figure out what to do with all that."

"Oh, yes, Ma'am. Thank you so very much, Ma'am." Jacques rolled over and jumped up, his eyes gleaming in a way that made Monica wonder if the relationship might have possibilities after all.

The boy opened one of the condom packages and slid it reverently over Kyle's cock. He took the bottle of lube, squirted some in his hand and applied it. Straddling Kyle's thighs, Jacques eased himself down onto Kyle's cock. His eyes rolled back in his head. Monica watched him bounce up and down while Kyle nibbled and licked and moaned with pleasure. Gripping the arms of the chair, Monica exploded. The intensity of the orgasm rippled through her over and over again until she had to insist Kyle stop.

"Ma'am, I'm afraid I can't hold out much longer." Still under the chair, Kyle's voice was muffled, so Monica pushed it back exposing his mouth and nose. "May I require the boy to stop?"

Monica laughed. "No, you've done well, boy. You may come."

"Oh, thank you, Ma'am. Faster, boy."

Jacques increased his speed and Kyle's body tensed. Within moments, he shouted out and thrust upwards, grabbing Jacques' hips. Monica smiled. She might not have gotten the exact scenario of her fantasies, but Jacques had demonstrated that he could provide excellent service to Kyle and entertainment for her. Surely, if she put her mind to it, she could come up with more ways the two of them could work together to satisfy her.

Searching

By I. G Frederick

"We could try putting a profile up on one of those online sites?"

Theresa scowled. "That's just ludicrous. I can't tell you how much time I wasted on that crap before I met you and I never connected with anyone worthy of a second date."

Richard shrugged.

"And we would never have met online."

He laughed. "True, neither of us would have given another dominant the time of day." He opened his arms and she settled in his lap, resting her cheek against the bristly hairs of his muscular chest. He kissed her brow and dragged his fingers through her waist-length, light brown hair. "But, I couldn't imagine my life without you. We just need to find a third before one of us takes the other's head off."

Theresa sighed. "We've attended every event within driving distance including half a dozen different Munch groups. Where are we going to meet this elusive addition to our family?"

33

"You always see the negatives. Why not look at the positive -- at least we find the same things attractive in a submissive. Imagine how much more difficult our search would be if we were both straight?"

She granted him half a nod.

"Let's go to the coast this weekend and we can relax, just the two of us, and get into the mood for Leather and Chains."

Theresa gave her husband a big grin. She already had two play dates lined up for the upcoming three-day event and hoped to find some of the other toys she enjoyed available for her amusement during the dungeon parties. "Okay. You're right, I really do need to hurt someone, but I wouldn't mind some time away with you, first."

Richard grabbed his cell from the table next to his big leather recliner and found the number for the Beach House in his contacts. "Lisa? Hi, it's Richard Stempson. Listen, I know it's short notice but I was wondering if you could find a room for me and my lovely bride for tonight and tomorrow night?"

He paused for several minutes and frowned. "I see. Can he cook?" He tilted his head. "Twenty percent off? It's a deal. I hope you have a wonderful visit to Seattle." He disconnected the call. "Lisa and Jennifer are leaving for a weekend in the Emerald City in a couple of hours. They had planned on closing down since it's still offseason. But, apparently Jennifer's nephew, who's a student at Oregon Culinary Institute, is house sitting and since we're regulars, she said she'd let us have the Rose Room at a discount." He nuzzled her neck. "We'll be the only guests."

She let her head fall back so he could kiss his way up her throat to her chin. "Sounds perfect, but I've got to get some work done first." Richard dragged his tongue along her jaw line and Theresa moaned. He pulled the strap of her bra from her shoulder.

Theresa was panting, but practicality overcame desire. "I need at least four hours on the computer before I leave the house. If you want to head out early enough to avoid rush hour ..."

Richard pressed his lips against hers then released her and guided her to her feet. "Why don't you get to it and I'll pack."

"Deal." Theresa pulled on jeans and a sweater and headed upstairs to her office.

 ○♄

When she shut down her computer at two-thirty, she found Richard had loaded the car and was waiting for her in the front room. "Looks like it'll be cool and foggy today, sunny and quite a bit warmer tomorrow. You might want to grab a jacket."

When Theresa joined him in the front seat of the Acura, he squeezed her thigh before backing out of the garage and hitting the remote to close the door. "I made six o'clock reservations at the Bite. That should give us time to check in and meet the nephew."

"As long as we don't get caught in traffic."

"Pessimist."

By the time he merged the car onto Highway 26, the rhythm of the windshield wipers and hum of the freeway beneath the car tires made it hard for Theresa to keep her eyes open.

"Take a nap, babe."

When she opened her eyes, Richard was turning from Highway 6 onto Highway 101. "Wanna stop in Tillamook?"

"No, if we drive straight through, we'll get to see the sunset."

Richard laughed and waved his left hand. "Given the clouds on the horizon, I'm guessing by the time we get to the coast all we'll see is fog, but we'll give it a shot."

When they rolled into Rockaway Beach, fog blanketed the road and Richard almost missed their turn. By the time he'd parked the car and extracted two overnight bags from the trunk, blackness engulfed them, and they cautiously climbed the steps up the hill to the house. The doorbell peeled through empty rooms. Only after Richard rapped the lion door knocker loud enough to startle the neighbor's dog into barking did a light turn on in the kitchen.

A tall, slender young man with curly brown hair opened the door and stepped aside to admit them. "Sorry, I guess I fell asleep studying. I'm Jesse." He stuck out his hand and Richard set down one of the cases to shake it.

"Richard and my wife, Theresa."

The boy's eyes widened as he stared at her and a puppy dog expression replaced the smile on his face. He had soulful brown eyes and a day's stubble on his chin.

Richard picked up the second case. "We know our way, don't trouble yourself."

"Oh, dear, I'm so sorry. You're just so beautiful." Without ever taking his eyes off Theresa, he reached out for the suitcases. "Please, let me take those up for you."

Richard shrugged and handed them over.

Jesse scurried over to the stairs, but then turned at the bottom and bowed. "After you, Ma'am, Sir."

Theresa gifted him with a smile, put her hand on Richard's arm, and walked with him up the wide, curved staircase. Jesse followed with the suitcases and set them on the luggage racks next to the fireplace in the Rose room. "Would you like me to turn this on for you?"

"Thanks, son, but we're going to go out for dinner first."

"Yes, Sir. Then I guess I'll see you in the morning. What time would you like breakfast?"

Richard laughed. "Your aunt doesn't usually give us a choice."

"I know, but since you're the only guests..."

"Then, why don't you serve at ten so we have time to take a walk on the beach before it gets crowded."

"My pleasure. I'll have the coffee on at eight, though, so you can have a cup before you head out, it you'd like."

After dinner, Theresa curled up on the plush pink love seat in front of the gas fireplace. Richard flipped the switch and squeezed in besides her. He stretched his long legs out toward the heat and wrapped his arms around her. "That boy seems rather smitten with you."

Theresa shook her head. "He's just a kid."

"I'll bet he's at least twenty-five."

"So?"

"Don't you think he's cute?"

"Yes, but he's probably Vanilla."

"I'd put money against 'nilla, too."

She shook her head. "I'm sure you'll find out more tomorrow. Right now, though, I thought we could pick up where we left off this morning."

Richard growled and ran his tongue along her chin. "Here, I believe?"

She moaned and let him push her sweater up over her breasts. He licked the skin above the lace of her bra, then unhooked the clasp to release her small, firm tits into his waiting palms. She sighed as he massaged them and licked between his fingers. Wiggling out of her sweater, she tossed it and her bra toward the chair on the other side of the bed. Richard teased one nipple with the point of his tongue and ran a hand down her back, stroking her fire-warmed skin.

Theresa unbuttoned his shirt and pushed it back over his shoulders so she could run her hands through the thick black hair on his chest and tweak his nipples with her thumbs, causing him to inhale sharply. He scooped her up in his arms and carried her to the bed, laying her across it and stretching out next to her. With his mouth attached to one nipple, he unbuttoned and unzipped her jeans, pushing them down over her slender hips. His fingers found their way between her thighs and nudged apart the silky dark curls covering her lips, seeking the moist heat within. She gasped, pushing up into his hand.

Chuckling, he stripped out of his own jeans and positioned

his hips between her legs. She wrapped her ankles around his waist, pulling him into her, relishing the piston-like strokes, the pressure his pubic bone exerted on her clit, the weight of his chest flattening her breasts.

He had one large hand on either side of her face and his tongue thrust between her lips with the rhythm of his pelvis grinding against hers. The tension built between her legs until she exploded, shaking in his arms. He chuckled again, increasing his pace and the force of his thrusts, making her come again before he grunted and shuddered.

When they caught their breath, he shifted so he lay on his back with her in his arms, her head resting on his shoulder. "Just think how delightful it would be to have that pretty boy cleaning up after me right about now."

She shivered with delightful anticipation. "I suppose you plan to proposition him over breakfast?"

"I think you'd get further, the way he stared at you..."

"And, what if he's straight?"

"Depends on how much he's willing to accept to get his sweet face between your beautiful legs."

Theresa laughed. "You're so wicked."

"Which is why you love me."

☙

Stopping in the kitchen for coffee the next morning, Theresa found the disarray a bit offputting. Jesse had pots and pans on every stove burner, pieces of a food processor strewn across the counter, flour covering every surface, and half a dozen bowls of various sizes containing a puzzling array of ingredients scattered about.

But the robust aroma of freshly ground and brewed java welcomed her and he filled two travel mugs as soon as he saw them.

"Black for me, sweetener and milk for the lady."

Jesse pulled the milk carton from the fridge along with two

more travel mugs. "My aunt said she starts breakfast with a fruit smoothie, but I made them to go in case you wanted something more than coffee ...." He set all four mugs on the breakfast bar. "Orange mango."

Theresa looked into his big brown eyes and smiled. "You sweet thing, how perfect. We'll be back in a couple of hours."

The boy twisted the bottom of his stained white apron in his hands and stared at his sneakers as she followed Richard out the front door, a metal mug in each hand.

Fog muted the colors of the surrounding houses. They picked their way across the gravel road to the path leading down to the beach. Richard stuffed one of his travel mugs in his jacket pocket and took her elbow, helping her balance over the rocks the size of laundry baskets. After they jumped down from the last boulder to the packed wet sand, Theresa took a swig of the full-bodied roast. She let the heat course through her limbs before strolling toward the thundering waves. The mottled white moon still hung low in the cloud-dark sky. Gulls left claw prints in sand smooth enough to reflect the tinge of color at the edges of the clouds.

She shivered in the brisk wind and Richard wrapped one arm around her shoulder, pulling her into his warmth. They meandered north, two of only a half dozen humans visible on the beach, sipping first their coffee and then the luscious sweet combination of tropics, citrus, and yogurt. The fog burned off and the wind died down. They shed their jackets and Richard carried them over one arm. By the time she'd emptied both her mugs, her boots dangled from Richard's other hand. The sand coated her bare feet with the warmth collected from the sun, but the wind kept goose prickles raised on her skin.

Just before they turned around, Richard spotted a pile of driftwood that resembled the remains of a raft. "Perfect picture." She laughed and obligingly lounged across the boards, while he captured the pose with the beach behind her.

When they returned to the Beach House, steam covered the windows. She squealed when Richard rinsed the sand off her feet with cold water from the hose. He stomped the sand off his own boots and they let themselves into the embracing warmth and tantalizing smells. He hung their jackets, set her boots and his own on the mat under the coat rack, and padded after her in stocking feet.

The kitchen was spotless, the dishwasher humming, and a fresh pot of coffee added its aroma to that of cinnamon, onions, apples, and butter coming from the stove and oven. The large oak oval table had two place settings at one end and a platter of fruit in the center.

"Did you have a lovely walk?" Jesse had replaced his apron, shaved, and combed his hair. "I hope it wasn't too cold. More coffee?" He lifted the pot.

Richard held out Theresa's chair and she pointed to the empty mug in front of her as she settled into her seat. "Please."

After filling both her and Richard's cups, Jesse added milk and a packet of sweetener to hers then scurried back into the kitchen. He emerged moments later with a platter of steaming apple walnut muffins which he placed between them.

Theresa only had time to inhale deeply of the cinnamon laced fruit and nut scents before Jesse returned again and set plates on the quilted placemats in front of each of them. "Careful, they're hot." In the center a ramekin held eggs, cooked with bits of red pepper and mushrooms, topped with Swiss cheese. Chunks of red potatoes sautéed with onions filled half the plate and two fat, juicy sausages adorned the other side.

Theresa added a muffin to her plate and broke off a bit of the top. "Yummy," she said after the flavors invaded her mouth.

"Very nice." Richard cut off a piece of the sausage and blew on it before popping it in his mouth. "How long have you studied at the Institute?"

"I have one more term to complete my culinary arts diploma."

"And what do you plan to do when you graduate?"

"Not sure, really. I'm .. well ... I don't ..." He turned and grabbed the coffee pot. "Here, let me top you off."

Theresa dipped a spoon into the egg dish and closed her eyes to enjoy the combined flavors of sweet peppers, earthy crimini, and savory cheese. She looked up to see Jesse staring at her, his brows scrunched together, his eyes pleading. "It's lovely, boy."

His face relaxed and he grinned. "I'm glad you like it, Ma'am."

She raised one eyebrow over the other. "You've a flair for cooking, but I'm wondering if you have any other talents?" She nibbled on a chunk of potato.

He trembled, the coffee in the pot coming dangerously close to spilling over.

Richard cleared his throat. "Put that down before you burn yourself, boy."

"Yes, Sir." He turned and, using both hands, set the pot back on the hotplate. "I'm sorry, Sir."

Richard tilted his head and looked at Theresa. She nodded. "Why are you apologizing, boy?"

He turned slowly, his lips pressed together so tightly they disappeared in a thin line across his pale face. "Your wife, is so beautiful, Sir," he whispered so softly Theresa had to stop chewing the succulent strawberry she'd lifted from the fruit plate to hear his words.

She laughed. "That still doesn't explain why you're apologizing." Picking up a whole sausage between two fingers, she pressed one end against her lips and slowly sucked in an inch of it while Jesse's eyes grew so wide she thought they would get stuck open. She chomped into the meat and licked the grease off her lips in slow motion.

Jesse was panting and even Richard's breath was heavy in her ear.

Chewing the sausage, she stared at Jesse's apron-covered crotch and wondered how tight his jeans had gotten. The boy sunk to his knees so gradually, at first she didn't realize he was moving. She took a sip of coffee. "Tell me, boy, what is it you wish most of all that you could do right now?"

Jesse collapsed on himself, burying his face against his knees. "You'll laugh," he sobbed.

Theresa softened her tone. "I can't promise you anything boy, except that. There's nothing you could tell me right now that would make us laugh."

Richard mouthed the words "I told you so" at her.

"You won't tell my aunt?"

"Of course, not, boy. What business is it of hers?"

He mumbled something against his jeans.

Theresa nibbled on her muffin. "Speak up, boy, I can't hear you."

Richard scooped up a fork full of potatoes, silently forming the word "feet" before putting it in his mouth.

Jesse lifted his face up high enough to clear his mouth. "I just want to kiss your feet." He trembled. "And, maybe suck on your toes. You have such lovely, delicate feet."

"I would love to have you worship my feet, boy. But, first I want to finish enjoying this delicious breakfast you've made us. Then I can move to a more comfortable chair and you can show me what other talents you have.

Jesse bolted upright, his eyes wide, his lips parted, his breathing ragged. "Really? But, you're married."

Theresa laughed. "That doesn't mean I'm monogamous." She took one last bite of sausage and pushed her plate toward Richard who exchanged it for his empty one.

"Do you know what a FemDom is, boy?" She snagged another strawberry from the fruit platter.

Jesse's pale skin blazed red. "Yes, Ma'am. May I ask, is your husband in service to you?"

She laughed. "No, he's also a dominant. And, we're searching for a third who would be submissive to us both." Suddenly, she realized why the boy had fallen apart when asked about his career aspirations. "What other schools have you attended, boy?"

He smiled. "I've studied massage, hair and nail care, and sewing, Ma'am."

She avoided acknowledging the smug look on her husband's face.

"My family thinks I can't make up my mind and pick a career. But, I was hoping to," he cleared his throat, "find a lady who would appreciate all the skills I've acquired."

"I see." She emptied her cup and raised her hand when Jesse jumped up and reached for the pot. Richard scraped up the last of the potatoes. "Shall we adjourn to the sitting room?"

Richard nodded.

"I'll go start the fire." Jesse tore down the hallway.

Richard rose and kissed her forehead. "He's cute. Reel him in for me, will you?" He followed her into the sitting room off the main entrance. Apparently Jesse had previously laid out a fire because he already had it blazing. He pulled one of two stuffed leather armchairs up in front of it. Theresa settled into the comfy cushions and waited while Richard looked at the other chair with a raised eyebrow. Jesse finally took the hint and pulled that one so it was facing hers. Richard plopped into it, stretching his stocking feet out toward the fire, his fingers intertwined on his flat belly, a self-satisfied grin on his face.

Jesse knelt in front of Theresa and she extended her right leg in his direction. He held her heel in his palm and dragged a warm finger along first one side of her cold foot and then the other. "So soft." He leaned forward, then looked up, pleading with his eyes.

Theresa smiled and nodded. He closed his eyes, pressed his lips against the top of her foot, and moaned. He kissed his way to her big toe and licked it, the heat of his lips and tongue warming her skin. She sighed. He grinned and sucked her toe into his mouth, caressing it with his lips and tongue until she purred. The expression on Jesse's face shifted and he adjusted his position so, without removing his mouth from her toe, he could massage her heel and the ball of her foot with his thumbs. She melted under the combination of eager nuzzling and skillful massage. By the time he finished with her other foot, more than her feet were tingling. Theresa's panties were damp and her hips wiggled of their own volition.

Richard must have left the room, but she didn't notice until he strode back in and stood next to Jesse, one hand behind his back. "Smell that delectable aroma, boy?"

Jesse's blushed. "Yes, Sir."

"How badly do you want to taste it?"

"Sir?"

"You clean, boy?"

"I was tested six months ago and I've not ..." He kissed one foot and then the other. "I mean ... I'm not..."

"I take your meaning, boy." Richard's voice was husky. He wanted the boy, badly. "You still haven't answered my question."

"What do I have to do?"

"I'll let you lick my wife's pussy as long as she can stand it and your tongue holds out."

"In exchange for?"

"Your ass is mine."

Jesse shuddered. He wrapped his arms across his chest, gripping his biceps. "I've never," he whispered.

Richard ran his hair through Jesse's curls, tilted his head back, and kissed him. "I'll keep that in mind."

Theresa unbuttoned her jeans and ever so slowly lowered the zipper. Jesse sobbed.

"Well, boy, you've got my wife all hot and bothered. One of us is going to have to go muff diving. Since you've pleased her, you can watch. Or ..." he dropped a towel, a bottle of lube, and a strip of condoms in Theresa's lap.

The boy rocked back and forth, trembling.

Balancing the condoms and lube bottle on one chair arm, Theresa stood long enough to put the towel on the seat cushion and slide her jeans and panties slowly down over her hips, her blouse dropping to cover her upper thighs. She sat back down and lifted her legs, pointing her toes at Jesse. He pulled her pants off by the legs and tossed her jeans on the chair Richard had vacated. He stared at the spot where her legs disappeared under white cotton.

She opened her knees just enough to release her scent. With a cry, Jesse dove forward, kissing the tender skin of her thighs while he untied his apron and unzipped his jeans. He inhaled deeply and Theresa threw one leg over the empty chair arm to give him better access. Richard's pants fell to the floor with a clunk of keys and wallet. He grabbed the condoms and lube as he stepped out of them. Jesse stuck out his tongue and ran it the length of her slit. Theresa sighed and slid lower in the chair.

Richard lifted Jesse's head by his hair long enough to pull the apron strap off his neck. When he released the boy's hair, Jesse dove back in. He thrust the point of his tongue into her and nuzzled her clit with his nose. Richard unbuttoned Jesse's shirt, removed it, then pulled away his jeans. Theresa enjoyed the view of the boy's firm ass sticking up in the air and Richard's sheathed cock pointing at her while Jesse nibbled on her nub with his lips. Overwhelmed with sensory stimulation, Theresa shuddered, her come gushing out over his face.

"Oh, yum," he muttered and licked and sucked and licked.

Richard knelt behind him, pouring lube into his hand. He slathered it over his rod and then shoved a lubed finger into Jesse's ass. The boy moaned and Theresa came again. By the time Richard had three fingers in the boy, he was squirming but he never stopped licking and sucking. She draped her legs over his naked shoulders and he pushed in so deeply, she worried he couldn't breathe. But his chest expanded and contracted in rapid gasps and his cock pointed down, straight and hard. Although not as thick as Richard, his dick was longer and Theresa thought he would make a lovely CBT toy.

Spreading the boy's cheeks, Richard eased himself into his ass, pushing until his pubes were up against the boy's skin. Jesse groaned, his breath hot against Theresa's clit. Richard slid back then pushed forward again. He moved slowly at first, but gradually he increased his speed until he slammed against the boy's ass. He leaned forward and reached around the boy, grabbing his nipples in between his thumb and forefinger. Jesse cried out, the vibrations sending Theresa off into another paroxysm. The boy shook and spurted all over the polished wood of the floor. Richard grunted and paused deep inside Jesse's ass.

When Richard eased out, Jesse sat back on his heels, his face in his hands, his shoulders shaking.

Theresa leaned forward and pulled him into her arms. He rested his cheek against her chest, his tears wetting her blouse.

Richard stripped off the condom. "I'll let it go this once, but next time you'd better get permission before you come, boy."

Jesse blinked. "Next time? Sir?" He looked up into Theresa's eyes and she smiled at him.

"We're looking for more than a sex toy, boy." Richard wiped his hands on the edge of the towel hanging from the chair. "And you've expressed a willingness to make yourself useful in a number of ways we find very attractive. If you're interested, we'd like to take you home and try you out."

Jesse hiccuped. "Yes, Sir, thank you Sir."

Theresa stroked his curls. "Why were you crying, boy?"

Without lifting his head from her chest, he wiped a finger under each eye. "I've never thought of myself as queer before."

"You may not be. Do you find Richard attractive?"

He shrugged. "Not really. I mean he's good looking, no offense, Sir. But, I think I'm straight."

"No offense taken, boy. Your orientation isn't really important, as long as you're willing to serve us both."

The boy nuzzled against Theresa, but didn't respond. His breathing slowed to normal before he spoke. "I think you've figured me out, already, Sir. I want to serve the Lady and I'll do anything to earn that privilege, even if that includes having sex with you. Is that acceptable?"

Richard laughed. "It's more than acceptable, boy, it's hot."

Jesse pushed himself up on the arms of the chair. "May I go get a rag to clean up my mess, Sir."

"Yes, boy, and bring us both some more coffee."

"Yes, Sir."

Jesse returned with a worn towel draped over his arm, carrying a silver tray. When they took their cups from the tray, he set it on a table, and wiped up the floor with the towel.

"May I ask what your plans are for the rest of the day? Will you be eating out or would you like me go shopping so I can make dinner."

Richard smiled. "We'll eat here, but I think the first order of business is to spend some time discussing our expectations and your hopes."

"Yes, Sir. May I clear the breakfast dishes first?"

"Go ahead."

Jesse staggered out of the room and Richard plopped back into his chair. "Guess you were right about online."

She snickered. "I suppose you anticipated something like this?"

He shook his head. "No expectations. Just the ability to recognize and the willingness to take advantage of whatever opportunity presents itself."

☙

After three hours of questions and negotiations, Richard settled down with his tablet to draft a six-month contract, Jesse headed for the grocery store, and Theresa luxuriated in silky, rose scented, steaming hot water. When the water turned cold, she emerged to the aroma of garlic, onions, and wine wafting through the house. She found a black, spandex, halter dress Richard had packed hanging in the closet and slipped into it, skipping underwear. Rummaging in her overnight bag, she found Richard also had packed a pair of black, patent leather shoes with three-inch spike heels. She put them on and went downstairs.

Richard, a glass of wine in his hand, leaned against the counter, watching Jesse scurry about the kitchen. When he saw her, he lifted his free arm. She stepped near and he pulled her against his shoulder, running his hand down her back to caress her ass through the thin fabric of the dress.

"I was just telling the boy that I sent him the draft contract via e-mail and I want him to take his time reviewing it after we leave. If we agree on terms, he can move in with us as soon as he finishes his last two months at the Institute."

"That sounds delightful." She accepted the glass Jesse offered and inhaled the fruity bouquet. "Will school occupy all your time or will you be able to visit?"

"I'll make time, Ma'am." Jesse flipped off the stove burners and lowered the oven temperature.

After dinner, Richard went out to the car and returned with a leather duffel bag. Theresa licked her lips. Jesse stared at it with a quizzical look on his face. Slowly, his eyes widened, his mouth opened, and his lower lip trembled. Theresa nodded and he dropped the pan he held in his hands into the sink with a clatter.

"Why don't you leave the dishes until morning, boy." Richard lifted the satchel.

Jesse stared at it, turning his head from side to side. "I don't know if ... I'm not sure... I've never ..."

Theresa stepped around the counter and ran a hand along the tight denim covering Jesse's lovely, firm ass. "Don't worry, boy. I'll be gentle." She slid her hand around to his crotch and grabbed his already hardening package. "At first." She stepped in closer. In her heels, she stood tall enough to reach his neck with her lips. "You do know the definition of a sadist, don't you, boy?"

"Ssssomeone who likessss to hurt people?" He was shaking, but he leaned back and she wrapped her arms around him, pressing her breasts against his back.

"Close. Someone who gets sexually aroused from inflicting pain."

Jesse turned, dropped to his knees, and wrapped his arms around her hips. "I want to please you, Ma'am."

She ran her fingers through his silky curls. "I know boy. And that turns me on."

He inhaled deeply. "What do you want me to do?"

"Well, the first thing you need to do is get rid of these clothes. In fact, I'd rather you not wear any for the rest of our visit. At home, you'll not be permitted to wear clothing except when you leave the house."

"Yes, Ma'am." He fumbled with the buttons of his shirt, but only got two undone. Untying his apron, he lifted it off his neck, then pulled his still-buttoned shirt over his head. Hands shaking, he set them on a chair and struggled to unfasten his jeans. He had them down around his ankles before he thought to remove his shoes.

Standing with his hands over his crotch in only his socks and his blue bikini underwear, he looked at her with those puppy dog eyes.

Theresa stepped close and pushed the elastic down over his hips. "You won't need these." She ran one finger along the side of his cock, smiling when it twitched and lengthened. She tugged one of his hands away from the other and led him out of the kitchen. He stepped free of his underpants and followed her to the staircase. Richard set the duffel on the fifth stair and unzipped it. He extracted a pair of leather cuffs and handed her first one then the other so she could buckle them around Jesse's wrists.

Wrapping a towel around one of the balusters, Richard clipped Jesse's cuffs together on the other side so he stood at the curve of the staircase with his hands bound together above his head. Richard handed Theresa a single tail and she cracked it to one side. Jesse jumped. Theresa ran her free hand along the soft skin of Jesse's ass and around to his rock hard cock. "Ready, boy?"

"I guess so, Ma'am."

Theresa stepped back far enough so she could swing the whip without touching Jesse. Slowly, she eased forward until the cracker kissed his skin. He flinched and her pussy muscles clenched. She stayed back for a dozen strokes, letting him get used to the sensation, then stepped an inch forward so the leather hit his skin hard enough to cause pain.

"Ouch, ouch, ouch, ooooohhhhhh." Jesse fell forward against the stairs and Richard reached through the balusters to steady the lad. Theresa could feel her juices trickling down the inside of her thigh.

She inched forward so the whip marked the skin on his ass and shoulders red, without raising welts. Richard held the boy's arms, keeping him from hanging from his wrists. She was breathing heavily now. Richard shook his head and Theresa let the whip fall to her side. She pressed her body against Jesse's back, crisscrossed with red marks. He moaned and she rubbed the damp fabric of her dress against his ass. The boy had sense enough to stick one leg back, allowing her to hump it, rubbing her clit against his thigh until she came with a shudder.

Richard chuckled and released his erect cock from his pants, dangling it in front of Jesse's lips. The boy obediently opened them, allowing Richard to slide inside the moist heat. Watching their new toy suck on her husband's dick turned Theresa on even more. She pulled her dress over her head, tossed it over the railing, and pressed her naked flesh against the heat of Jesse's back. The boy wiggled his ass and she raked her fingernails across the red marks from her whip.

As soon as Richard filled the boy's mouth, she unclipped the cuffs, grabbed Jesse's hair, and pulled him to his knees. She threw one leg over his shoulder and shoved her dripping pussy into his face. Glassy eyed, the boy sucked on her nub until she gushed all over his face. Richard appeared behind her, reaching around to toy with her nipples. She took a fistful of Jesse's hair in each hand to steady herself. With a cry she came again and fell back into Richard's arms.

"Can you make it up the stairs, boy?"

"I think...I'll try."

By the time he laid her across the bed, Richard was hard again. He thrust himself inside her and she was vaguely aware of Jesse crawling into the room on all fours. While her pussy spasmed around Richard's cock, she stretched one hand out to Jesse and he knelt beside the bed, pressing his head against her palm so she could stroke his curls. When Richard finally spent himself inside her, Theresa was trembling in ecstasy. Richard stretched out beside her, one hand on her breast.

"I've made a bit of a mess, boy. Clean her up."

"Yes, Sir." Jesse worked his mouth up one thigh and down the other, sucking up the sticky combination of her cum and Richard's. Then he licked everything he could from her bush and slurped Richard's semen from her cunt. She opened her legs and Jesse's lips attached themselves to her clit, sucking on it until she exploded, her body shaking in Richard's arms.

When she finally stopped trembling, she grabbed Jesse's curls and pulled him up to lay besides her. Richard reached across her and fondled his head while Jesse clung to her, his arms wrapped around her waist. Theresa fell asleep embraced by her husband and their submissive, grateful that their search was over.

Taking Control

By I.G. Frederick

Melanie opened the front door and cringed when she heard the crack of the whip, the slap of leather on naked skin, and Theresa's moan. *Why?* she asked herself for the fiftieth time. *Because you love her, and the bastard won't let her see you any other way.* Repulsed and excited by what she would find at the bottom of the stairs, horrified by her own continued participation, Melanie slipped off her clothing. She hung her jeans, cotton panties, bra, and t-shirt on the coat rack and ignored the leather corset dangling from the hanger on the doorknob. Pausing at the top of the stairs, she took a deep breath before descending.

The rough wood of the steps under her feet gave way to the cold cement of the basement floor and Melanie shivered. Inside Ron's dungeon -- a dank corner of the basement with only large metal eye hooks and wooden racks adorning the faux stone walls--Theresa dangled from the ceiling. Leather restraints, clipped to short chains, encased her wrists. She gripped the chain in her hands, so the metal links cut into

53

her palms. Sweat beaded up on her pale forehead, and her long blond hair spilled over her shoulders and covered her luscious breasts. The whip cracked again and another red mark appeared across her back. From the number of welts crisscrossing the creamy skin of Theresa's slender back and wonderfully firm ass, Melanie guessed the two had been at it for twenty minutes or more. Typical of Ron to tell her to show up long after he planned to start. Still, better to arrive and see the marks than watch him apply them.

Ron tossed the six-foot-long bullwhip into the corner and dropped into the leather director's chair he kept for watching. His paunch spread over his meaty thighs, hiding his pitiful penis. Scabs covered his legs; Melanie had never garnered the courage to ask what caused them. The only muscles she could see bulged in Ron's right arm.

"You can take her down now."

Melanie approached Theresa and kissed away the tears that trickled from her bright green eyes. When the younger woman stopped shaking, Melanie unbuckled the restraints and left them dangling from the chains. She put one shoulder under Theresa's arm and took her weight while walking with her to the stained mattress on the floor in the corner of the dungeon. They eased down together, and Melanie kissed Theresa hard, thrusting her tongue deep into her mouth. Theresa sucked on it and the two fell back onto the mattress, their breasts pressed together, their arms wrapped around each other. Melanie let her hand drift down Theresa's back, across her ass, stopping to squeeze the taut muscles, and then caressed the silky smoothness of her thigh.

Melanie pulled her lips from Theresa's mouth and kissed her way along the line of her neck stopping for a moment at the base of her throat before moving down to her breasts. She licked from chest to dark areolas until Theresa's nipples begged to be sucked and Melanie obliged. When both breasts glistened, Melanie moved lower and Theresa wriggled in anticipation, her sweet musk beckoning. Melanie inhaled deeply and then nuzzled Theresa's shaved lips apart with her nose. She tried to position her own cunt over Theresa's face, but, as usual, Ron pushed her hips aside and inserted his limp cock into Theresa's mouth. Melanie tried to ignore the slurping sounds, concentrating instead on licking Theresa's clit, hoping to make her come so hard that she would bite off Ron's useless prick.

Although Theresa bucked and pushed her hips into Melanie's face, Ron just grunted and moaned. Melanie listened in vain for a scream of pain or even a whimper of discomfort. Theresa reached down and gave Melanie's hair a tug, urging her to bring her face up out of the depths of delight. Melanie resisted, gripping Theresa's thighs, trying to stay in the heaven of her scent, the taste of her dripping juices. As much as Melanie needed the release that Theresa's tongue would bring, the thought of what would come with it nauseated her. But, Theresa pulled until Melanie's head hurt. Since Theresa took pleasure in her pain, she sometimes forgot not everyone could.

Melanie kissed her way back up to Theresa's face and gripped her tightly, hoping to keep her mouth busy. She guided Theresa's hand down to her slit, but the younger woman didn't take the hint and dragged her tongue down Melanie's torso. Melanie turned her head away from the stench of Ron's crotch, but he pinched her nipple until she cried out. She hated herself for accepting his abuse, but couldn't give up the pleasure that went with it. Trying not to gag -- not that he had much to gag her with, but he tasted of rancid leather -- she kept her mind on the delectable sensations Theresa created.

Ron came before Melanie could -- without ever getting hard -- and rather than take his spunk in her mouth, she turned before he spurted so it dribbled down her chin and across her shoulder. Once he stopped bothering her, Melanie could relax and enjoy Theresa's efforts. The woman had an amazing tongue. Theresa flicked it across Melanie's clit, thrust it deep inside her cunt, and rimmed her asshole until Melanie cried out and her entire body trembled with the strength of her orgasm.

The two women snuggled for as long as Ron would let them, Melanie sobbing in humiliation against Theresa's shoulder. When he dragged Theresa by her hair over to the whipping cross, Melanie pushed herself off the mattress and hurried up the stairs, her stomach churning. She pulled on her clothes, trying to ignore the screams that emanated from the basement. She hesitated for a moment, found a scrap of paper in her jeans pocket, and grabbed a pencil off Ron's kitchen table. The thoughts she had wanted to share so long committed to paper, Melanie examined Theresa's short, slutty leather skirt and sheer blouse, then secreted the note in the inside pocket of the leather jacket that matched the skirt. She patted the jacket, hoping Theresa and not Ron would find her message, then checked her appearance in the mirror on the wall. After running her fingers though her short blonde hair, Melanie dragged her sleeve across her chin to remove the remains of Ron's spew. Watery blue eyes set close together over a too-broad nose stared back at her. She shook her head, checked the zipper on her jeans, and let herself out of hell.

Melanie stared at the computer monitor and gripped the mouse, the pointer wavering over the submit button. The fetish sites asked for way more information than the one where Ron had found Melanie when he went looking for a woman to partner with Theresa. Theresa's photograph and profile had intrigued Melanie, but, she learned later, the correspondence all came from Ron. He had answered Melanie's questions and set up their first meeting. Melanie hoped she could use the same tactics to find what she wanted. Still, she answered only the required questions, disheartened by how little she actually knew about Theresa's life outside Ron's dungeon.

Since their first date, when Melanie fell in love with Theresa's sweet disposition and bubbly outlook on life, Ron had refused to let them spend any time alone together. Melanie never felt comfortable talking to Theresa in the dungeon knowing he listened to every word. She yearned for a repeat of their first night together, alone in Melanie's apartment, savoring the softness of one another's skin, the smell, the taste of each other. Melanie still remembered her gut punch reaction to the news that Teresa belonged to Ron and did what he told her. Now, the need to get Theresa away from Ron's clutches inspired Melanie to post what she had written.

The next day, Melanie found her fetish-site mailbox inundated. Even though she hadn't included a photograph, more than three hundred men had viewed the profile she posted, forty-five had added it to their hot lists, twenty-three had sent a wink, and seven had written e-mails. Melanie only responded to the e-mails of local men under forty who had included a photograph. As more and more e-mails flooded the inbox each day, she recruited one of her straight friends to help her select the ones who appeared the most handsome.

She peppered those with questions about their proclivities, preferences, limitations, and requirements. When the correspondence and the language the men used discouraged Melanie, she remembered Ron forcing himself into her mouth. That, and the desire to punish him for taking advantage of Theresa's naïveté, gave Melanie the strength to interrogate the men on the telephone, screening thirty candidates down to six. Now, she just had to wait until Theresa found the note and, Melanie hoped, called.

$\mathcal{C}$

"Melanie?" When the call finally came; when she heard Theresa's warble on the other end of the telephone; Melanie had to cover her mouth to refrain from sobbing.

"Yes, Theresa. Will you let me help you?" Tears streamed down Melanie's face.

"I don't know. I think you're wrong, but..."

"Theresa, I know I'm not wrong. I've found dozens of very good looking guys your own age who can do everything for you that Ron does." Melanie took a deep breath. She had told herself she could live knowing Theresa had found someone to make her happy even if it meant giving her up, but the prospect still twisted a knot in her stomach. "And, Theresa, they can still get it up and fuck you if you want. You don't have to wait until I come over to get off."

"I would still want to see you, Melanie," Theresa whispered. Melanie suppressed another sob of relief. "Will these guys you want to fix me up with, will that be okay with them?"

"Of course it will, sweetie. You know I love you. I'll do absolutely anything I can to make you happy." Including talk to strange men about their sexual preferences, Melanie thought to herself. Theresa would never understand just how difficult that had been.

She heard Theresa swallow. "Do you just not like Ron or do you not like any guys?"

"I particularly don't like Ron, but I don't like any guys. Why?"

"How come you went to the trouble of finding me one?"

Maybe Theresa did at least sympathize. Melanie smiled. Then, she sighed. "Look, Theresa. I know I wrote that I understand your need for pain. The truth is I don't, but I've learned to accept it. I also know you're not a lesbian; that you could never be satisfied with just me or even with just a femdom. I love you. I want you to be happy. I can't stand to see you abused by that impotent old fart. He's what, twenty years older than you? I know he introduced you to the lifestyle, but that doesn't mean you have to stay with him."

"But, I need a Master."

"I know, sweetie. And I've got half a dozen, buff, good looking, thirty-something guys eager to accept you as their slut."

"Me?"

"You're beautiful, Theresa. Any Dom would be thrilled to own you."

"But Ron..."

"Fuck Ron. Oh wait, he can't get it up to fuck, can he? He wouldn't know something beautiful if it sat on his face. Trust me. These guys are ready to fight over which one gets to own you, just based on my description."

"You probably made me sound a lot prettier than I am."

"No, actually, I talked more about your submissiveness. They know your measurements, that you have long blong hair, green eyes, and a cute little fairy tattoo on your ass. But that's about it."

"And they want to meet me?"

"All at once or one at a time. You pick."

Theresa gasped. "All at once?"

"Sure, they know you get to make the final selection. They think they've got hot stuff and they're willing to put it in front of you."

"Could I ... do you think... Oh, Melanie, I've always fantasized about being used by a whole roomful of men at the same time."

Melanie closed her eyes. "I'll make the arrangements as long as I don't have to watch."

"But, I'd want you to be there when I meet them."

"I'll invite them all over here. You can look them over. But if you're going to have sex with half a dozen men, I don't want to see it." Melanie shuddered. "I'll just leave, okay. You can stay here as long as you want with as many of them as you want. I've checked them all out. They're all clean and safe. None of 'em gets into really gross stuff like scat or watersports or blood. You can let me know if you don't like any and I'll make them leave when I do."

"I can't believe you're doing all this for me."

"I'm doing it for me, too. So I don't have to put up with Ron's disgusting cock in my mouth if I want to spend time with you."

"Thank you, Melanie. Even if none of these guys collars me, I want you to know I really appreciate all your effort."

A week later, Melanie helped Theresa prepare for her encounter. The younger woman waited for her suitors on her knees in Melanie's living room, naked except for the leather binders that imprisoned her arms behind her back, inch-wide straps traversing her narrow shoulders to cross above the delectable mounds of her breasts. When Melanie finished tying the laces, she licked Theresa's nipples until they stood erect and wet.

When the first Dom arrived, Theresa's eyes widened and the tiniest smile played across her lips. Even Melanie could tell that the tall man, she thought his name was Tomas, spent hours in the gym. Muscles rippled across his chest when he removed his shirt and he dropped his pants to display powerful thighs and a cock that, only partially erect, put Ron's to shame.

"No one touches her until I give permission," Melanie told the man.

He looked her up and down, but didn't respond. Melanie wore leather pants and a breath-restricting black bustier that she had rented from a costume shop. By presenting herself as Theresa's Mistress, Melanie figured she would have more authority in eliminating any of the Doms that Theresa didn't like. These last few weeks had been an eye-opener. Melanie had learned more about fetishes, S&M, and "the lifestyle" than she had ever wanted to know. But she also had discovered more respect for herself than she had thought possible.

Two of the six candidates left the apartment with Melanie a half hour later -- the two, she noted wryly, with the smallest peckers.

When Melanie returned to the apartment after the agreed-upon four hours, only Tomas remained. He lounged on the sofa, fully clothed. Theresa, her arms still bound behind her back, lay on her side on the floor. Red marks covered her ass and thighs and she had spunk in her hair, on her face and her tits, and dripping out of her cunt and her ass. When she saw Melanie, Theresa grinned wider than the clown on the last hole of miniature golf. A thick, golden slave's chain encircled her neck.

Tomas stood. "Theresa has agreed to wear my collar. You're welcome in my dungeon any time she's there. I'll watch the two of you slurp each other. I'll fuck Theresa wherever I want while you're there, but I'll never touch you. If the two of you want to spend time together when I don't have use for her, she's free to do so."

He rose to his feet, towering over Melanie. "Since you're my girls' lover, I will consider you a member of my leather family. In a nutshell, that means if someone's giving you shit you can reach out to me and I'll make sure they stay off your case. You'll be invited to, but not obligated to attend, my occasional family gatherings. Under the circumstances, I'm not going to ask that you contribute to the family in any way. But, I'll let you know if an opportunity for you to help out comes along and if you're so inclined..." He shrugged and let himself out of the apartment.

Melanie dropped to her knees and unlaced the binders. She pulled Theresa into her arms, ignoring the sickening sweet spooge smell. "Happy?"

"Ecstatic." Theresa leaned her head against Melanie's shoulder. "You have to let me find a way to repay you for all you've done. I really like Tomas. We talked for a long time after the others left. He's amazingly nice -- believes he should treat all women, even sluts like me, as if we were ladies in public." She laughed, a trill that was music to Melanie's ears. "He won't make me do things I don't like. He smells so much better and tastes so much sweeter than Ron. And this afternoon really was a fantasy come true. I enjoyed it so very much." Her eyes took on a dreamy look and she licked her lips. "I had one in my ass, one in my cunt, and the other two taking turns in my mouth. All at the same time."

Melanie didn't want to hear more details. "I'm glad you're

happy, Theresa. But I just want to make love to you, the two of us alone, no one watching."

"No."

Melanie's stared at the woman in her arms, wondering what made her so cruel.

"I mean, I want to do that, too. And, I still want you to come over sometimes to Tomas' dungeon. I know you don't understand this, but I love having a cock in my mouth when you're eating me out. And I want to get rammed from behind while my face is buried in your pussy." Theresa placed one palm against Melanie's cheek. "But making love to you, the two of us alone, is something I'm looking forward to as much as you. I want to do something that's special just for you."

Melanie shook her head. Listening to Theresa's exaltations about the afternoon, she had forgotten the woman had said that she wanted to repay her. "I'm sure we'll think of something." Melanie smiled and kissed Theresa, thrusting her tongue in between the other woman's lips. She pulled free and laughed. "You can let me tell Ron."

Theresa pulled away and stared at Melanie. "You're kidding?"

"No, I'm not." Melanie pushed herself up onto her knees. "You were there willingly, but that old bastard tormented me for months, without my consent, and it's about time I stood up to him, don't you think?"

Teresa pulled on her nipple and stared at the floor. "I'm not sure willingly is the right word," she whispered. Then, she smiled. "You realize, you actually would be doing me a favor by telling him. That was the one thing I tried not to think about this afternoon."

"Look, Theresa. Despite his contentions to the contrary, the man really doesn't own you. You don't wear his collar and you never even signed a contract with him, did you?"

Theresa shook her head.

"Then, let me have the pleasure of telling him that his treatment of me has backfired in a big way. The old fart will probably never get another sub as pretty as you." Melanie ran her fingers through Theresa's sticky hair. "But first, let's go get you cleaned up so we can enjoy each other." She stood, pulled Theresa to her feet, and led her into the bathroom.

Melanie stripped off her clothes, tossing them into a heap in the corner, pulled open the shower door and reached inside to turn on the taps. When she got the temperature right, she nudged Theresa, stepped in behind her, and pulled the door closed. Theresa stood under the showerhead, her eyes closed, water sluicing over her face and through her hair. Melanie reached behind her for the shampoo and enjoyed the touch of Theresa's breasts nuzzling her own.

Theresa's hair always smelled of lavender, Melanie hoped she wouldn't mind generic drugstore brand. She massaged the soap into Theresa's scalp, pulling her from the water stream so she could spread the lather through her sticky hair. Unable to resist, Melanie kissed Theresa. Theresa's hands cupped Melanie's breasts and her already erect nipples hardened. Together they moved back under the shower and Melanie rinsed the soap from Theresa's hair while Theresa ran her hands up and down Melanie's back, pausing to squeeze her ass.

Melanie fumbled for the bar of soap and used one hand to paint Theresa's backside while the other hand followed and enjoyed the silky sensation of soapy skin. They traded the bar back and forth, rubbing soap on each other's backs, breasts, legs, arms, necks. With the water cascading over their heads, Melanie kissed Theresa again, thrusting her tongue deep in her lover's mouth delighting when the younger woman drew her hand up between Melanie's thighs probing between her nether lips. Gasping, Melanie let Theresa stroke her clit with slick fingers until she trembled in ecstasy. When she finally stopped shaking, Theresa released Melanie and stuck her finger in her mouth. "Mmmmm, I think I want more of that." She winked, turned her back on Melanie and rinsed herself off. She stepped out from the water, pushed Melanie under it, and used her hands and tongue to make sure Melanie had no more soap on her skin.

When Melanie turned off the taps, Theresa pushed open the door and reached for the towel hanging on the wall next to the shower. She rubbed Melanie's hair with it, then patted her down with the soft terrycloth before handing the towel over. Melanie made quick work of drying Theresa and led her by the hand into the bedroom, eager to resume their love-making. She pulled back the blanket while Theresa kissed the back of her neck. When she turned, Theresa leaned forward until they both fell onto the bed, laughing. Theresa, who had landed on top, kissed her way down from Melanie's neck, to her breasts, and, dragging her tongue across Melanie's belly, found her way between her legs. Melanie pulled at Theresa's hip and was delighted when the younger woman maneuvered her cunt over Melanie's face.

Melanie breathed deep of the honey and plunged her tongue inside as far as she could thrust it. For only the second time, she could enjoy the taste and smell of her lover while relishing the pleasure Theresa gave with her own tongue. Her hands on Theresa's ass cheeks, Melanie nuzzled, licked, and sucked until they both trembled. Holding on, Melanie kept her mouth busy while the orgasm tore through her. She could feel Theresa's cunt spasming with her tongue and realized her lover wasn't the only one who had gotten to live out her fantasy today.

Family Ties

By I.G. Frederick

Katherine pulled aside the lace curtain to watch the woman helping the twins from a Volkswagen van that had seen better days. Normally her slave picked up his son and daughter from his wife's home on the other side of the river for their weekend visits. But Naomi was heading to Oregon Country Fair and wanted to drop the tweeners off a day early on her way south.

A consummate hippie, Naomi had feathers poking out of her unruly red hair and beads of various colors wrapping her arms up to her elbows. Her earth-mother halter dress exposed creamy white skin. Katherine hoped she planned to stay out of the sun this year.

When Luke stepped out of the front door, the kids raced toward him screaming "Daddy," so loudly Katherine could hear them through windows closed against the July heat. The words Luke exchanged with his spouse were lost to her, but the longer they spoke, the more enamored Katherine became of Naomi.

65

The woman's skin radiated wholesomeness, her turned up nose and pouty bottom lip made Katherine want to turn her over her knee. She would love to redden her rounded ass with a paddle. Her wonderfully perky breasts, that probably would be on display all weekend covered only in body paint, would look lovely bristling with clothespins. Katherine sighed. One of the main reasons Luke had left Naomi was because she had no interest in BDSM and he could no longer live without it.

The van pulled out of the driveway and stuttered down the hill. Katherine wondered if it would make it all the way to Eugene. At that moment, Elizabeth and Edward burst into the room.

"Show your respect," Luke commanded.

Elizabeth curtsied and Edward bowed. Katherine opened her arms. The two flung themselves into her embrace and started rattling off everything they hoped to do while visiting. Katherine smiled and let them know what she and Luke had planned for the weekend: a visit to the Berry Festival on Saturday and a trip to the zoo on Sunday. As expected, Elizabeth clapped her hands at the mention of the zoo and Edward immediately listed all the berries he hoped to taste.

$\mathcal{C}$

When the van chugged into the driveway just before midnight Sunday, Luke had already tucked his progeny into their beds. He opened the door to Naomi before she could ring the bell and wake them.

"Sorry, I'm late." Her pale skin had burned lobster red.

"Boy, go draw your wife an oatmeal bath."

Naomi, still wore the same dress she had on Thursday, but the beads were missing. She kept her arms akimbo. "Thank you, Ma'am. But, I'd better get the kids home."

Katherine glared at Luke until he bowed and scurried out

of the room. "Your children are asleep. It's too late to disturb them. And you look exceedingly uncomfortable. Elizabeth tells me your bathtub is in need of repairs. You may take advantage of mine."

A tear drifted down Naomi's cheek, leaving a trail through dust on skin that probably hadn't been washed since Katherine had seen her last. "It's hard." She clapped her hand over her mouth.

Katherine crooked a finger. "Come here, child. You may confide in me. And, if you wish, I won't share anything with Luke unless it's going to adversely affect your children."

"Of course it'll hurt them." She grimaced. "You live up here in your great big house and don't have a clue what it's like to struggle to survive." Another tear followed the first.

Katherine raised one eyebrow and Naomi put her hands back over her mouth.

Luke returned and bowed. "Naomi's bath is ready, my Lady."

Katherine set her book on the table next to her chair, rose, and extended a hand to Naomi. "I'll take care of her. You may get ready for bed. You'll need to leave early to take the children to day camp and I don't want you to be late for work."

Naomi ignored Katherine's hand but followed her up the stairs to the second floor and into the hall bathroom. "May I use the toilet first, Ma'am."

Katherine leaned against the wall. "Go ahead."

Naomi's blushed visibly, despite her skin's already reddened tone, but she pulled up her skirt and sat on the commode. She stared at the floor until she rose, lowered the lid, and flushed. "I suppose you're going to watch me take a bath as well."

"We need to talk and this is as good an opportunity as any. Fortunately, I don't have to get up early."

Naomi washed her hands, turned her back to Katherine, and untied her halter top, letting her dress slip to the floor in a cloud of dust. The sunburn completely covered her backside, including her ass. She put one foot in the water and gasped.

"Ease in slowly."

"It's cold."

"Hot water would only further damage your skin."

Naomi lowered herself into the tub and exhaled. "Thank you, Ma'am."

"Why don't you tell me what's wrong." Katherine sat on the toilet seat lid.

Naomi covered her face in her hands and sobbed. "I don't know what I'm going to do. The bank's kicking us out at the end of the month. I still haven't found a job. I don't have security deposit and first and last month's rent to pay for an apartment. And, even if I did, most places won't take kids. Those that do get snapped up before I even get a chance to respond to their ads."

Katherine shook her head. "What in the world? Why haven't you let us know you were in trouble sooner?"

A tapping on the bathroom door startled them both. Naomi sunk further into the water.

"Yes?" Katherine called out.

Luke opened the door, a bottle of lotion in one hand, a bundle of fabric in the other. "I brought Naomi some aloe lotion and something to put on." He hung one of Katherine 's old robe's from the hook on the back of the bathroom door. "I made up the guest room in case she's not up to driving home."

Katherine accepted the bottle and he took the opportunity to kiss her fingers. "Good night, my Lady."

When he left, closing the door behind him, Katherine turned back to Naomi. "Perhaps you should tell me exactly what's going on."

Naomi shook her head.

Katherine stared at her.

"Luke didn't tell you that the bookstore went out of business?"

"He didn't have to tell me, I read it in the news."

She shrugged, rippling the water so it exposed her dark delectable nipples. Despite suckling two children, her breasts were still firm, although the nipples were elongated.

"I've applied to every bookstore in town and other retailers as well. The only offers I've gotten were for part-time, minimum-wage jobs that wouldn't even give me enough to make the current mortgage payments, never mind get caught up on the ones I've missed."

She wrapped her arms across her breasts. "I don't suppose you could take the kids?" Staring at the faucet, she nudged at the overflow face plate with her toe. "I know you hide stuff from them and having 'em around would put a crimp in your 'lifestyle.'" She released her arms to draw air quotes. "But I'm not gonna have any place for them."

"And, where will you live?"

Naomi's chin came to rest on her chest. She closed her eyes. "In the van."

She looked so vulnerable, her red hair drifting in the water caressing her blistered shoulders. Katherine had to resist the temptation to take advantage of her predicament.

Naomi shivered and Katherine held out a towel. She rose, the water dripping off her skin. The water in the tub had turned murky red with dirt. Katherine pulled the towel out of Naomi's reach. "Perhaps you'd like to wash some of the dust off?" She flipped open the drain and drew the shower curtain closed.

When she turned off the water, Naomi reached blindly around the edge of the curtain and Katherine let her have the towel.

"Ouch."

"Just pat yourself dry. Don't rub. Then we can put on some of this lotion."

Naomi followed her instructions, but winced every time the terry cloth came into contact with her damaged skin. Katherine couldn't help getting turned on by the other woman's pain. "What about the checks I send you every month?"

"I spend that on the kids, of course." Naomi reached for the lotion bottle and slathered some on her arms, breasts, and still flat stomach. "You wouldn't believe how much it costs just to feed Edward."

Given the amount the boy ate on his weekend visitations, Katherine had no trouble envisioning that as a major expense.

"Then there's ballet lessons and shoes for Elizabeth, trumpet lessons and band uniform for Edward. Every sport, every extra-curricular activity has fees, uniforms. Luke paid for day camp, but I still have to come up with gas to get them here every day. Even though Luke covers the health insurance premiums, I still have to fork over co-pays anytime one of them needs to see a doctor or take medication." Naomi smeared lotion on her legs and turned her back to Katherine. "Do you mind?"

Katherine smiled and filled her palm with lotion. She spread it across Naomi's backside, lingering on the luscious globes of her ass.

"When I was working full time, my salary paid the mortgage and the utilities and usually covered gas for the van and sometimes I even had enough for a night out with friends when Luke had the kids."

Katherine closed the top of the lotion and handed Naomi her robe.

"Every once in a while the end of the month came too soon, but usually I managed to stay on top of the basics." She shrugged. "Unemployment only pays two thirds of what I was earning. I've gotten further and further behind every month. The kids have given up their lessons. If something breaks it doesn't get fixed. But, I still can't make the mortgage payment every month, not and keep the lights and the water turned on."

Opening the bathroom door, Katherine led Naomi to the guest room at the opposite end of the hall from the children's rooms. Naomi sat cross-legged on the bed.

Katherine settled in the chair under the window. "Of

course the children can stay here as long as necessary. Fortunately, the house is big enough that Luke and I can keep our lifestyle separate from them."

Naomi tilted her head to the side and one sleeve of her robe slid off to reveal a very red shoulder. "What exactly is your lifestyle? Luke has hinted that ... well, before he left, he wanted to ... but ..." She blushed again.

"You know that I own Luke? He's my property?"

Naomi's eyes widened and she turned her head from one side to the other and back.

"He obeys me and I take responsibility for him."

Naomi stared at her. "What exactly does 'take responsibility for him' mean?"

"I make all decisions regarding his welfare. I decide what he eats, when he exercises, what he wears, where he works, how his money is spent, etc. I don't tell him how to be a father to his children, but I do advise him in that regard. And I decide how much of his income he can afford to send you to cover their needs."

Naomi's lower lip trembled. "I wish I had someone to take care of me like that."

Katherine harumphed. "Aren't you a bit too much of a free spirit to give total obedience to anyone?"

Naomi hung her head. "Freedom comes with a price and I'm seven months behind on that price. Besides, having kids eliminates any free spirit urges rather quickly." She looked up. "I love Luke dearly, but having to take care of twins and him was just too much."

Katherine leaned her head against the chair's upholstered back. "Why exactly did you and Luke split?"

"He didn't tell you?"

"I want to know your version."

Naomi sighed. "Neither of us really was prepared for parenthood. As time went on, I realized Luke needed as much mothering as the kids. Hell, Elizabeth is more mature than either of us. I just couldn't manage him and them both. So

I asked him to leave." She covered her face with her hands. "And, the twins are the ones ending up without a home." She sobbed.

Katherine sighed. "Your children have a home, my dear. The question is will you?"

Naomi peaked at her through her fingers. "Are you saying there's room for me here, too?"

"For a price. I would love to have a female slave as well as a male. But, that's the only opening in my household."

Naomi dropped her hands into her lap and took a deep breath. "What exactly does that entail?"

Katherine folded her arms across her chest. "Complete and total obedience to me. Following my protocols at all times. Serving me in any way I command, including sexually. And I *am* a sadist. I beat my slaves, torture them."

"And the downside?" Naomi whispered.

Katherine grinned. "My dear, if you don't see a downside in what I just described there isn't one. But, Luke said he left because you had no interest in BDSM."

Naomi pressed her lips together. "I had no interest in hurting him. Or being his Mistress. And, after the kids were born I couldn't drum up much enthusiasm for sex, at least not with him. Luke was the first, and only, man I had a long-term relationship with. Before that, I mostly dated women."

"And since?"

"Who has time to date with two kids and a full-time job? For the last ten years, the only time I get laid is at Country Fair." Naomi raised her head for the first time since she sat on the bed. Tears pooled at the corners of her eyes. "Can I try being your slave for a bit and see how ... if ... whether?"

Katherine laughed. "Slavery hasn't been legal in the United States since 1863. If I accept ownership of you, it's only for as long as you consent to be owned."

"Or you get tired of me and throw me out."

"We've known each other now for what, five years?"

Naomi nodded.

"You're the mother of my slave's children and I suspect he still loves you, as well. I find you exceedingly attractive and if you're willing to serve as my slave I don't see any reason I would get tired of you." Katherine rose. "For now, you need to get some sleep. After Luke takes the kids to day camp, we'll discuss this further."

"Yes, Ma'am. Thank you, Ma'am."

"You may call me my Lady. I prefer that to Mistress."

Naomi smiled. "Thank you, my Lady. Good night."

$\mathcal{T}$

Naomi read the slave contract three times then picked up the pen and signed it. Katherine had written it for six months with the option of making it permanent at that time. After she scrawled her name across the bottom of the last page, Naomi knelt in front of Katherine.

"I require my slaves to be naked at all times unless we have company. That includes the children, of course. But when they're at school or away for any other reason ..."

"Yes, my Lady." Naomi stood, removed the robe, draping it over a dining room chair, then returned to her knees.

"Much better." Katherine fastened a slender gold chain around Naomi's neck. "This is a collar of consideration. If, after six months we decide you will become my slave permanently, I will put a collar around your neck that can't be removed without bolt cutters."

Naomi touched the chain with two fingers. "Thank you, my Lady. How may I serve you?"

Katherine strode toward the stairs. "Come with me." She led Naomi up two flights to the suite on the top floor of the house. When they were both Inside, she locked the door and stepped to the built-in bookcase along the wall opposite the door. Removing the *Complete Works of William Shakespeare*, she reached inside and pressed the combination that released the latch. One third of the bookcase turned ninety degrees, revealing another room behind it.

Naomi gasped, but she dutifully followed Katherine into the dungeon. Her eyes widened when she saw the right wall covered with leather, wooden, and metal implements of bondage and torture.

Katherine opened a cabinet on the wall that separated the dungeon from the bedroom and extracted a bottle of massage oil. "Since your skin needs to heal a bit before I can play with you, I will allow you to give me a massage.

"Thank you, my Lady." Naomi removed Katherine's robe and looked around until she found an empty hook to hang it from.

Katherine pulled a sheet from a drawer and handed it to Naomi who used it to cover the massage table that, along with a bondage rack and spanking bench, lined the wall opposite the cabinets. Laying on her stomach, her forehead resting on her arms, Katherine listened while Naomi poured oil into her hands and rubbed them together. She started at Katherine's shoulders and worked her way down her back, rubbing oil into her skin. Katherine sighed with pleasure.

Naomi's massage was more sensual than therapeutic. She used her forearms to caress Katherine's back from the just above her ass to her neck. Before she applied oil to Katherine's behind, Naomi kissed her way up, down, and across the sensitive skin. Katherine moaned.

Using her fingers, her palms, her arms, Naomi stroked Katherine's rear end, legs, and feet. When Katherine rolled over onto her back, Naomi applied oil first to her legs, then her arms, and belly. When she reached her breasts, Naomi switched to her tongue, bathing every inch of Katherine's ample mounds and sucking on her nipples. Katherine grabbed Naomi's hair and guided her mouth down to where she needed it most.

"Oh, thank you, my Lady." Naomi inhaled deeply and then gently pulled apart Katherine's nether lips. She proved to be as talented with her tongue as she was with her hands.

Licking the length of Katherine's slit, she nuzzled her clit with her nose. She wrapped her lips around Katherine's nub and teased it with her tongue until Katherine trembled, lifting her hips off the table, and crying out with delight.

Naomi wrapped her arms around Katherine's back, holding on and working her tongue deep into her pussy until Katherine cried out again. She grabbed Naomi's hair and pulled her up onto the table and held her, her soft breasts pressing into Katherine's side.

$\mathcal{C}$

Naomi retrieved the twins from day camp. By the time Luke returned from work, Edward was sprawled across the sofa and Elizabeth curled up in the arm chair in the living room, their noses buried in books. Naomi bustled about the kitchen from which the enticing aromas of frying onions, garlic, ginger, and coriander emerged.

Luke knocked on Katherine's office door. "My Lady?"

She nodded. He entered, closing the door behind him, and knelt next to her chair.

"My Lady, am I permitted to know why my children are here on a non-visitation day and why my wife is apparently preparing dinner?"

Katherine set her glasses on her computer keyboard and turned her chair to face Luke. "When I accepted you into my service, I permitted you to stay married to Naomi so she could continue to receive health insurance through your employer and other spousal benefits. I send her generous checks every month. But, even with your income I can't afford to support two households. And, now that Naomi's not working she can't make up the difference."

Luke hung his head, his chin resting on his chest. "I was worried that she couldn't keep up with the mortgage payments," he whispered. "But, I was afraid to ask. I thought she would let me know if she needed help."

"She asked me if the children could live with us. But she doesn't have anywhere to go herself. As part of discovering all this, I've also learned that apparently you weren't entirely honest with the reasons for your split with her."

Luke tilted his head to one side. "My Lady?"

Katherine put on her sternest face, enjoying her slave's discomfort. "You told me you left Naomi because she had no interest in BDSM."

He threw himself forward and embraced her feet. "I didn't lie, my Lady. I love Naomi. I would adore serving her. But, whenever I tried to broach the subject ..."

"You failed miserably. Because your wife is a submissive."

Luke pushed himself up and stared at her with wide eyes.

"I've taken Naomi under consideration as my slave. Since she's not currently working, I will turn most of the household chores over to her. That will give you the opportunity to tackle some of the projects that have been set aside while you tried to juggle everything. This weekend I expect you to go with her and help her pack up anything she wants to keep from your house and dispose of anything else."

Luke sat back on his heels, he head tilted to one side.

"By fall we should know whether this arrangement will succeed so we can decide where to enroll the twins for school. I'll set Naomi's unemployment check aside until then. Worst case scenario she'll have enough to get an apartment."

Luke's chin trembled. "And, the house?"

"Under water. In foreclosure. Easier to walk away then try to straighten out the mess." She smiled. "I'm relatively confident that I will enjoy Naomi's service and we can make this family work as a unit. Since this house is big enough for all of us, I see no reason to take on the burden of another. Let the bank straighten out the mess."

"But, my Lady, if the children live here I can't serve you naked."

Katherine sighed. "Unfortunately. But, you and Naomi will take your clothes off when you come up to the third floor and since the children aren't allowed up there..." She shrugged. "It's not ideal, but I can live with it."

"Yes, my Lady."

"I'll expect you to make sure Naomi is thoroughly trained in my protocols for inside and outside of my sanctuary upstairs. Teach her how to manage my home the way I prefer it."

"Yes, my Lady."

Luke jerked when they heard a knock at the door. He jumped up and opened it to admit Naomi who dropped to her knees. "My Lady, dinner is ready. Where would you like me to serve it to you?"

"We'll all eat at the dining room table, girl. I need to inform the children they will be staying here and we probably should make a habit of eating at least one meal a day as a family."

$\mathcal{T}$

After the twins had been tucked in by both their parents, much to their delight, Katherine was pleased to have two naked slaves kneeling at the entrance to her suite. Naomi's skin had gone from lobster red to reddish brown and she no longer winced when she brushed against something. Luke looked rather pasty next to her, some work in the garden would improve his appearance. He had gotten a little pudgy around the middle, too. Katherine needed to make sure some of the extra time he'd have was spent at the gym.

Luke stole glances at his naked wife and his cock already pointed straight out. Katherine chuckled. She had no intention of letting it go anywhere near Naomi -- she planned on keeping that particular bit all to herself -- but the girl had done well her first day and deserved a reward. Setting her book down, she rose from her chair and stood in front of the dungeon entrance. Luke jumped up, locked the bedroom door, and entered the combination behind the Shakespeare volume. They both followed her inside.

Katherine pointed at a selection of leather wrist and ankle cuffs and Luke retrieved two pairs of each. She waited while he fastened the smaller set to Naomi's wrists and ankles and helped her fasten the larger to his. Katherine pushed a button that lowered one of the suspension hooks from the ceiling, clipped each pair of cuffs together, and looped them over the hook. Before recoiling the chain, she turned her two slaves so they stood back to back. Naomi's head rested against Luke's shoulder.

Katherine held the button until Naomi's hands were straight and his elbows bowed out. She grabbed two spreader bars from the wall and attached them crisscrossed so each bar was clipped to the left ankle of one and the right ankle of the other.

When she removed a four-foot signal whip from the carousal stand in the corner, Naomi turned a rose-tinted shade of pale. "My Lady?"

"Yes, girl."

"You know I have no experience?"

"Of course, girl. And don't hesitate to vocalize -- this room is sound proof." Katherine grinned at Naomi's discomfort and Luke's obvious arousal. She stepped back and cracked the whip over her head. Luke closed his eyes and Naomi trembled. Katherine swung the whip from side to side, gradually moving in so Naomi could feel it cross the air in front of her. Then she flicked it so it tweaked Naomi's nipple. The girl yelped, but the smell of her arousal reached Katherine's nostrils and she saw moisture gleaming on her thighs.

Circling her slaves, Katherine snapped the whip so it struck tits, bellies, and the tip of Luke's prick. Naomi thrust her hips forward, so Katherine let the whip smack her mons. Despite assurances that their children couldn't hear them, neither made a sound. They both kept their lips pressed together, their eyes scrunched closed.

Katherine traded the signal whip for a six-foot bullwhip. She wrapped it around their waists, their hips, and chests, alternating which one the cracker struck. When they both had red marks crisscrossing their skin, she hung the whip and lowered the hook until Luke could remove Naomi's cuffs.

While the two extracted themselves from their restraints, Katherine grabbed a riding crop, stripped out of her clothes, and made herself comfortable in the chaise lounge under the window. The slaves crawled toward her and Katherine snapped her fingers at Luke, pointing to her toes. She held out a hand toward Naomi. Luke obediently crawled to one end of the leather chaise and licked first one toe and then another. Lapping and sucking, he slowly bathed each and every digit.

As soon as Naomi was close enough, Katherine grabbed her by the hair and pulled her to her chest. Naomi's mouth gave Katherine's breasts the same attention Luke devoted to her toes. Katherine moaned and leaned back, reveling in the sensations of hot lips and moist tongues caressing her skin.

Occasionally she landed the crop on whichever ass she could reach. But the sensations were too intense, making it difficult for her to lift her arm. She eventually let the crop drop from her fingers, but not before she planted several additional red welts on each of them.

Luke worked his way from her feet to her ankles, up her calves, toward her thighs. Naomi concentrated on Katherine's large breasts. By the time Luke reached her cleft, Katherine was panting and dripping. His tongue found her nub and she exploded. She grabbed Naomi by the hair, pulled her up, and took her long, firm nipple in her mouth. Biting down, gently at first, Katherine pushed her hips toward Luke's face and sunk her teeth into Naomi's breast while Luke's tongue sent her into another shuddering orgasm.

She grabbed his hair and lifted his head. "Get me my strap on."

"Yes, my Lady." He crawled toward the cabinets and returned with her leather harness, a double-sided purple dildo, a bottle of lube, and a string of condoms. He buckled the straps into place, eased one end of the dildo into her soaking pussy, covered the other end with a rubber, and then slathered it with lube.

Katherine directed Naomi to lie on her back and pushed Luke's face between her legs. She stepped behind him and eased the sheathed end of the dildo into his ass. All three moaned at the same time. Naomi wriggled under Luke's expert attention, while he squirmed as the dildo plunged in and out of his ass. Her own movements rubbed the dildo against her clit and g-spot, bringing Katherine close to the edge again.

"Oh, God, please, my Lady." Naomi begged between clenched teeth.

Katherine laughed. "You may come, girl." She and Naomi both shuddered and moaned.

"May I, as well, my Lady?" Luke asked, even though he knew better.

Katherine pulled out and unbuckled the harness, letting it fall to the carpeted floor.

"Absolutely not, boy." She dropped next to Naomi on the chaise, pushing Luke away with her feet. "Go clean up the toys."

He bowed his head. "Yes, my Lady."

When he disappeared through the bookcase, Naomi asked, "Forgive me if I'm being impertinent, my Lady, but is Luke being punished?"

Katherine chuckled. "No, he's not allowed to come more than once a week, although I may make him wait a couple of extra days for asking when he knows he's supposed to wait until at least Wednesday."

Naomi swallowed. "And may I ask, how often will my Lady allow me to come?"

Katherine shrugged. "Depends on how good you are. I permit females to come more often than males. If you do as well as today, you may earn daily release."

Naomi grinned. "Thank you, my Lady. I think I will enjoy serving you very, very much."

Said the Unicorn: Now That We See Each Other

By I.G. Frederick

Tessa waited on her knees for Master to finish his phone call. Although she obediently looked down at the floor, she couldn't help admiring him through her lashes. Master's powerful legs, muscular chest, and well-formed biceps left her weak-kneed and in awe of his dominance.

A strand of her long blond hair drifted over her shoulder. Tessa tossed it back. Master didn't like anything covering her breasts, even her hair which he loved to play with and pull. She straightened her back and thrust her tits forward so her hair would stay behind her shoulders.

Finally Master set the phone on the table next to his big leather armchair. "Now, my pet, where were we?"

81

"You said you had a request to make of me when the phone rang, Sir."

He chuckled. "It was a rhetorical question, pet. I do remember." He put one finger under her chin and tilted her head back, giving her permission to look in his eyes.

Deep blue, surrounded by dark lashes, they drew her in, making it difficult to concentrate on his words.

"Do you know what a unicorn is, pet?"

That has to be a trick question. "A mythical beast that looks like a white horse with a single horn in the middle of its forehead?"

He laughed and she dropped her chin to her chest. *Wrong answer.*

"That's one definition. But, in this case, I'm referring to an even rarer creature, one that's more difficult to catch. A unicorn is a bisexual woman willing to join an existing couple and become part of their family."

Tessa bit her lip trying to prevent the tears that sprang to her eyes from spilling over. She gasped for breath and tried to push words out of her mouth. "Permission to speak, Sir?"

"Of course."

"Master is displeased with me? I don't serve him adequately? Please, Master, tell me what I've done wrong, how I can do better, why he wants someone else?" A single tear trickled down her cheek and she felt it hanging at the end of her chin before it splashed onto her breast.

Master opened his legs and pulled her between them, cradling her head against his tight abdomen. "You've done nothing wrong, pet, I'm not at all displeased with you. Rather, I think you're progressed far enough in your training that it's time to start looking for a third."

She sobbed.

He stroked her hair. "Pet, you've always known I'm poly, I told you that from the very beginning."

I thought I could learn to serve you so well you wouldn't want another slave.

"I just wanted to concentrate on training you, make sure you were comfortable with my protocols, before I introduced another girl to the mix."

Her tears had soaked his shirt and she tried to pull away so she could go get him a dry one. But, he held her against him, one arm wrapped around her shoulders, the fingers of the other running through the long blond strands that hung halfway down her back.

"Don't worry, pet. You'll always be first in my heart. If you'd like, I'll let you find the slave you want to be your sister, as long as I approve of her, of course."

"I don't want a sister," she wailed, protocols forgotten. "I'm straight."

"I will give you some leeway in how you interact with your sister slave." His stern tone sent an arctic chill through her heart. "But, I have no intention of limiting myself to one woman. I explained that when you first offered yourself to me."

"I can't, I just can't." Tessa almost choked on her tears.

"Do you want some time to think about this?" He pushed her shoulders back until she sat on her heels much further away from the comfort of his arms than she wanted to be.

"Please, Sir."

"You may go to your room."

Tessa hung her head, pushed herself to her feet, and backed away.

U

Tessa ordered a mocha and found an empty table in the small coffee shop that had become all too familiar over the past few weeks. She checked the time on her cell. Blind date number fourteen would be late in three minutes. Master insisted on punctuality and tardiness was on Tessa's list of behavior that made someone unsuitable. She admitted that list had gotten rather long, but Master was being patient. If she had to accept another woman in his home, she wanted to make sure it was someone she could at least be friends with.

The bells over the glass door jangled and a stunning brunette entered. Tessa held her breath. She really didn't need someone more beautiful to compete for Master's attention. The woman had thick black hair almost as long as Tessa's. Black eyeliner accented startling blue eyes under flawlessly arched eyebrows that slashed across creamy skin. Pink lipstick shone from perfect cupid bow lips and black nail polish gleamed from surprisingly short, but perfectly shaped, nails. She wore a black halter top that showed off an impressive cleavage and leather pants accenting slender hips. Tessa wondered how Master would feel about the industrials in the woman's right ear. She also wore a collection of leather bracelets on both wrists and large silver tear-drop earrings.

The woman approached Tessa's table just as the barista called out her name, so she couldn't exactly pretend to be someone else. "Hi, I'm Marie. Let me get that for you."

Marie paid for her own drink and brought Tessa's mocha to the table, setting it in front of her with a subtle bow. She pointed to the chair across from Tessa and gave her a querying look. Tessa nodded and she sat down.

"I hope you don't mind me saying, you're so very pretty."

Tessa blushed.

"I love your hair. And your eyes. I would definitely call that emerald green."

The barista called her name and Marie went to get her coffee. She stood by her chair until Tessa nodded before she sat down again.

"I can't tell you how excited I am at the prospect of becoming part of a family again. I'm so very tired of being alone."

Tessa sipped at her rich chocolate-coffee combination. "You never did say what happened to your previous family."

"I don't like to talk about it. I was driving. Even though it wasn't my fault ..." Marie dropped her eyes. "Master sat beside me in the passenger seat and my sister slave, Laura, behind him." She drank some of her coffee but even after she set the cup back down she didn't speak. After a minute, she said. "The man who hit us was drunk. He ran a stop sign and t-boned the passenger side." All color had drained from her face. She toyed with the handle of her coffee cup. "Master and Laura were killed instantly. I was in the hospital almost two weeks."

Her lips trembled. "He spent less than a year in jail." She looked up, tears glistening in her eyes. "He took everything from me and he didn't even go to prison."

Tessa reached across the table, put her hand over Marie's, and squeezed gently. Marie looked up and the corners of her mouth lifted slightly then dropped again. "Master and Laura were married and he didn't have a will. Her family took everything, the house, the second car, all the furniture. They left me with nothing, just my clothing." She grabbed her cup and gulped down more of her coffee. "It's been almost two years. It still hurts, but I think I'm finally ready to move on." She turned her hand so she could hold Tessa's.

Tessa sipped her mocha. "Do you have questions for me?"

Marie nodded. "How did you meet your Master?"

Tessa smiled. "I was a gift. My first Master trained me but never collared me. He said he was too old for me. Master was his protégée. He gave me to him for Master's birthday with the condition that if Master didn't keep me, he would return me. I'm so grateful Master has found me worthy of his collar." Tessa touched the leather band buckled around her neck, the tag that proclaimed his ownership nestled in the hollow of her throat.

Marie smiled. "What a lovely story. You're so fortunate. I had several bad relationships before I met Master and Laura." She pressed her lips together. "One man claimed to be a Dom, but Master said he was just an abusive stalker."

Tessa suppressed an urge to pull Marie into her arms and comfort her."Would you like to come home and meet Master?" Marie would be the first girl she introduced to Master. She hoped he liked her as much as she did.

Ul

When Tessa entered the vestibule off the garage, she pulled off her jeans and tank top, hanging them on the hooks on the wall, and kicked off her sandals. She turned to find Marie had already removed her top and was unzipping her leather pants. She had a black thorny rose tattooed on her breast. Tessa hesitated, but Master had never said how he expected her to introduce any prospects to him and he didn't allow her to wear clothing in his house. Perhaps Marie stripping was for the best.

She led the other woman into Master's study and knelt on the plush carpet at his feet, waiting for him to put down his book. Marie fell to her knees on Tessa's left and bent over so her face rested on the carpet her arms above her head. She had a tat of a jaguar striding across her kidneys on her back.

When Master peered at her over his reading glasses, Tessa said, "Sir, may I present Marie. She's interested in serving you and being my sister slave."

"Good girl." Master reached forward and grabbed a fistful of Marie's hair, pulling her into a kneeling position. He pulled some of Tessa's golden hair across Marie's ebony locks. "Nice. I like the contrast."

He turned to Marie. "Tessa's obviously comfortable enough to bring you home. She shared your experience with me before the two of you met and she can train you to meet my needs. So, the only question is how good are you?"

Marie crawled forward and Tessa cringed. This was the part she knew would hate most -- watching anyone else please her Master. Marie unzipped his fly and extracted his already semi-erect cock from his boxers. "Thank you, Sir." She kissed his glans and licked the length of his rod from pubes to tip until it stood straight up.

Weighing his heavy sack in one hand, she grasped the base of his cock in the other and plunged her lips down his shaft to her fingers. Master gasped and Tessa had to bite her lip to keep from bursting into tears.

Master stroked Marie's long, black hair. He crooked a finger of his other hand at Tessa and she crawled over to him, grateful he was even aware of her presence. While Marie's head bobbed up and down, Master grabbed a hunk of Tessa's hair and pulled her up so he could suck on her tit. He released Marie and grabbed Tessa's other nipple, twisting it until she gasped. So slowly that she didn't notice at first, his teeth sunk into the one in his mouth. Her breathing grew heavy and she could smell her own musk as well as Marie's. Hers had much more of a rich vanilla aroma than Tessa's own that Master always described as honey sweet.

When Master came, Marie swallowed every drop. Tessa tried not to pout, but her lower lip crept out from her upper.

"Good, girl." Master patted Marie on the head. "Now, I want to see you two together."

"But, Sir?" Tessa sank back onto her heels.

"It's okay, pet." He reached out his hand and she rested her cheek against his palm. "You don't have to go muff diving since you're straight. You can close your eyes and pretend it's whoever you want between your legs."

"You, of course, Sir."

He chuckled and looked at Marie who had a big grin on her face.

"Thank you, Sir." She opened her arms and Tessa sighed and crawled into them. Marie's touch was delicate and Tessa was surprised to discover she liked the feel of another pair of tits pressed up against her own. Marie ran her hand up and down Tessa's back and stroked the sensitive flesh of her ass until she gasped. Tilting Tessa's chin up, Marie touched her lips to Tessa's. At first, she kept them tightly together, but Marie teased with her tongue until Tessa relented and parted them.

Marie tasted of coffee and peppermint. She ran her tongue along the inside of Tessa's lips while fondling one breast until she was gasping for breath. Easing her back onto the carpet, Marie kissed her way down Tessa's neck to her breasts, tickling them all over with the tip of her tongue and suckling on her nipples. Tessa suppressed the urge to wriggle her hips. Master didn't allow that.

Finally, Marie made her way along Tessa's belly to her cunt. Marie pulled her lips apart and dragged the full length of her tongue through Tessa's slit. She almost screamed. The woman had a piercing near the back of her tongue. When the ball hit Tessa's clit, she had to dig her fingers into the carpet to keep from coming. "Please, Sir," she gasped.

"You have permission to come as much as you want when you're with this one, pet."

Tessa let go and her body shook under Marie's expert ministrations. She convulsed on the carpet as Marie tormented her clit and thrust her tongue deep into Tessa's cunt. Vaguely aware of Master's scent, Tessa opened her mouth and he pushed his cock between her lips. Unable to give him the attention he deserved, she just kept her mouth shaped like an O so he could face fuck her while Marie kept stimulating the orgasm that wouldn't end. Tessa was still trembling when he shot his load deep into her throat and she had to concentrate on swallowing so she wouldn't choke.

"Nice." Master lifted her up into his arms and held her against his chest.

Marie wrapped her arms around Tessa and Master, pressing her breasts against Tessa's back. Tessa clung to Master, but no longer questioned her place in his heart. He had room enough for both of them, and as long as she came first with him, she would find room in hers.

Acknowledgements

This book would not have reached your hands without the help of many dear friends and colleagues. I thank my readers and supporters, especially Cindy, my proofreader, editor, and best friend. Thanks also to all those who have served me, well and ill, over the years. I have learned something from each one of you and I hope that you find what you seek.

Other fiction
by I.G. Frederick includes:

Complicated Couplings

Four sexy stories about tangled twosomes

"If You Love Someone" — *Tara leaves her husband to move in with Nathan, but he abandons her after a few months. When he returns, begging her to take him back, life and love look very different.*

"Commiserate" — *The same man dumped them both. When they commiserate, they discover more in common than an ex-boyfriend.*

"Passion's Price" — *Richard steals Gina's heart from three thousand miles away. But, when he moves across the country, her intensity and passion for life drive him away.*

"Lunchtime Lover" — *Both married, they started their affair with the promise never to fall in love. Then Lisa's divorce becomes final.*

www.eroticawriter.net/ComplicatedCouplings.html

Cougar Conquests

Beautiful older women on the prowl and the sweet young cubs captured by their allure

"Benjamin" — A chance meeting at a munch in a tiny town leads Benjamin to an opportunity for training. But, Lady Gina tries to end the relationship rather than emotionally torture herself.

"Festival of Eros" — The handsome young man followed her around all evening, behaving like the perfect submissive ... until she learned his identity.

"Paddles" — A biker bar with no bikers? The decor, name, and patrons of a bar in a small Eastern Oregon town puzzle William who just stopped in for a beer. Then the owner introduces him to the secrets of this very special tavern.

"Starting Over" - When her pet walked out on her, she stayed away from parties because it hurt to watch other women playing with their toys. But, a friend coerces her into attending a unique event.

"The Cougar and the College Boys" — Alone in the woods, hours from Portland, Tess discovers four college friends staying in a nearby cabin. The boys invite her to share their campfire, their dinner, and ...

www.eroticawriter.net/CougarConquests.html

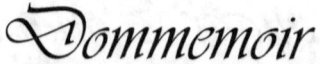

WARNING:

This book changes women's attitudes about relationship dynamics, forever.

In Geneviéve's journey of discovery she dabbles in the BDSM lifestyle which forces her to recognize and acknowledge her true nature. Her memoir, woven together with that of a male slave, draws the reader into an intense odyssey of sexual expression triumphing over sexual repression while delivering fascinating insight about a different kind of love.

"The aptly titled Dommemoir *delivers on so many levels... It quickly sucks you in and envelopes you in the bondage of its spell...* Dommemoir *is a character study that breathes complex and compelling life into its hero, the devastating Lady Geneviéve and the fortunate submissives who worship at her feet... placing you in the delicious bondage of its dark and compelling landscape..."*

Larry Brooks, USA Today bestselling author of Darkness Bound **and** Bait and Switch

www.eroticawriter.net/Dommemoir.html

Eleanor & Mick
A journey of sexual exploration and insight

In five sizzling hot stories, Eleanor seeks refuge in a small town on the Oregon Coast and befriends her younger neighbor. He captures first her heart and then her submission, taking her on a journey of sexual exploration and insight.

"Salt for His Wounds" — When Eleanor's ex-husband shows up begging for a second chance, she asks her young, gorgeous next door neighbor for a favor and Mick takes advantage of the opportunity.

"The Mercantile" — Eleanor attributes Mick's detachment to the difference in their ages, but Mick confesses a need for kink. Afraid of losing him, Eleanor reluctantly consents to bondage and pain.

"The Things We Do for Love" — When her gorgeous girlfriend visits Eleanor on the coast, Mick's obvious attraction troubles her. But, Liz only has eyes for Eleanor.

"Paid in Full" — Mick's army buddy finds Eleanor hot and makes a deal with Mick. But, if Mick really loved Eleanor would he let another man have sex with her?

"Renovations" — After Mick spends a month renovating their garage, Eleanor discovers he built in a few surprises.

www.eroticawriter.net/EleanorMick.html

Fork In The Road

Changing people's lives, and relationships
in three pairs of sexy stories

"Said the Unicorn" — Tessa dedicates herself to her Master's service, so his determination to add another woman to their family devastates her.

"Proposals" — The evening appears perfectly arranged for him to pop the question. But, Christopher's proposition takes Geraldine on an unanticipated sexual adventure.

"Winners & Losers" — When he finally walks away from the blackjack table, Jeffrey finds someone worth gambling on.

www.eroticawriter.net/ForkinRoad.html

Ladies in Love
Six sizzling stories of Lesbian Lust

"Empty Seat" — *Laura offers Alex a nightcap as thanks for help with a presentation to a prospective client. But they never order drinks.*

"'Aunt' Grace" — *Jen needed a place to stay in Portland and turned to her father's stepsister. But, she found so much more than she ever dreamed possible with her "Aunt" Grace. Second Place, National Leather Association: International John Preston Short Story Award.*

"Spa Date" — *Dismayed that she introduced Sam to the woman who betrayed her, Julie tries to fix her up again.*

"Taking Control" — *To free the woman she loves from a horrid sadist's perverted games, Melanie must set aside her own aversion to men.*

"Dental School" — *How can Cindy flirt with the beautiful blonde dental instructor while her mother propositions the student examining her teeth on Cindy's behalf?*

"Commiserate" — *The same man dumped them both. When they commiserate, they discover more in common than an ex-boyfriend.*

www.eroticawriter.net/LadiesinLove.html

Lessons Learned

Sometimes you need more than love

Four sizzling hot FemDom love stories about women who come to terms with their dominant sides and discover that makes them more attractive to the men they love.

"Tea Party" — What if the first time your best friend drags you to a FemDom "Tea Party" you see your former boyfriend serving canapes naked?

"Blind Date" — How do you respond when you find your ex-husband hanging out at the restaurant where you planned to meet your "Blind Date"?

"To Serve" — If you love a vanilla woman and you only want "To Serve," how do you introduce her to the lifestyle without scaring her away?

"Change in View" — What if a "Change in View" alters the attitude of the man you mentored so he could find his perfect Mistress?

www.eroticawriter.net/LessonsLearned.html

Love Hurts

but in a good way
five steamy stories about the dark side of love

"B&D Trainee" —Online, Xavier promised to make his B&D fantasies come true. But, had he jumped in over his head?

"Knife Play" — Seeking a knife he saw online, Jack inadvertently found himself in a room full of pain and bondage contraptions. He almost turned around and left, but a beautiful woman taught him a different way to appreciate blades.

"Pussy Whipped" — Eric knew nothing about BDSM, but purchased a ticket to a fundraiser to help out his friends. When Miranda asks him to "play," he discovers exactly what those four letters mean.

"The Auction" —He attended the auction with only one goal — to acquire a very special whip. But an offer to try it out proved irresistible and he discovered sometimes events, and women, can exceed one's expectations.

"FemDom Fairy Tale" — A FemDom's offhand remark about a photograph at an erotic art show draws a handsome man's attention. But, when two dominants find each other attractive, which one chooses to kneel?

www.eroticawriter.net/LoveHurts.html

Second Chances

Six sexy stories about getting a second shot at the gold ring

"Back to School" — An admin error forces Jordan and Dennis to share a dorm room. Older than their classmates, they decide to stick together. But Jordan's past threatens to keep them apart.

"Gordon" — When the cover model of her latest book walks into the coffee shop where she writes, Lenore embarrassingly calls him by her character's name. His reaction confounds her.

"Spa Date" — Dismayed that she introduced Sam to the woman who betrayed her, Julie tries to fix her up again.

"Salt for His Wounds" — When Eleanor's ex-husband shows up begging for a second chance, she asks her young, gorgeous next door neighbor for a favor. Mick takes advantage of the opportunity.

"Proposal — Tangled Webs" — The evening appears perfectly arranged for him to pop the question. But, Christopher's proposition takes Geraldine on an unanticipated sexual adventure.

"Starting Over" — When her pet walked out on her, she stayed away from parties because it hurt to watch other women playing with their toys. But, a friend coerces her into attending a unique event.

www.eroticawriter.net/SecondChances.html

When Two's Not Enough

Seven sexy ménage stories

"Tribal Fusion" — Whenever and wherever he dances, Dominic collects propositions, but the Lady Lenore's proposal takes him by surprise.

"Two Brothers" — A divorcée in a flashy sports car attracts the attention of two young virgin brothers visiting the "big" city of Boise.

"Honeymoon" — Although she expected to honeymoon aboard a cruise ship, Allison finds herself sailing on a private yacht staffed by an incredibly beautiful couple. Believing her new husband wants to hide his older, less attractive wife, makes it difficult to enjoy the hedonistic delights offered in paradise.

"Jail Bait" — Serena wants Joshua to pop her cherry, but he won't touch her because of her age. When her birthday finally makes it legal, he arranges for a very special celebration.

"Nikki's Birthday" — Even someone happy in a monogamous relationship might find the gift of a hot, new toy for an evening of decadence incredibly exciting. (Inspired by a real birthday present given to a lovely little bi-sexual, genderqueer slave.)

"Market Boy" — When a beautiful Domme offers Jack

the opportunity to serve at a party for her friends, he responds too quickly and too eagerly, getting more than he bargained for.

"The Cougar and the College Boys" — Alone in the woods, hours from Portland, Tess discovers four college friends staying in a nearby cabin. The boys invite her to share their campfire, their dinner, and ...

www.eroticawriter.net/TwoNotEnough.html

Young & Eager

Barely legal but hardly innocent

"Two Brothers" — A divorcée in a flashy sports car attracts the attention of two young virgin brothers visiting the "big" city of Boise.

"Teachers Pet" — Trapped at an all-girls' school in the middle of nowhere, Sabrina tries to get her hunky teacher to bust her cherry.

"Arresting Development" — Bethany went out with Officer Rick to avoid a speeding ticket, but discovered she enjoyed getting "arrested."

"Jail Bait" — Serena wants Joshua to pop her cherry, but he won't touch her because of her age. When her birthday finally makes it legal, he arranges for a very special celebration.

www.eroticawriter.net/YoungEager.html

Or visit
http://eroticawriter.net/
to find links to individual stories
and additional collections
and

For darker, edgier fiction
look for books by
KORIN DUSHAYL
The Darker Side
of Intimacy
transgressivewriter.com